*Sara and Lillian are desperately in
need of husbands. And Mr. Fellows,
Mr. Hudson, Mr. Alistair,
Mr. Reising, Mr. Basingstoke and
Lord Allingham are all
campaigning for Parliament . . .*

*SWEET AND TWENTY—
A delightful Regency Romance
where anything can happen.
And does.*

# Sweet and Twenty

### JOAN SMITH

FAWCETT CREST • NEW YORK

*SWEET AND TWENTY*

Published by Fawcett Crest Books, a unit of CBS Publications,
the Consumer Publishing Division of CBS Inc.,
by arrangement with the author.

Copyright © 1979 by Joan Smith

ALL RIGHTS RESERVED

ISBN: 0-449-23818-0

Printed in the United States of America

10  9  8  7  6  5  4  3  2  1

# Sweet and Twenty

# 1

SIR Gerald Monteith performed one act in his life not motivated entirely by self-interest—he married a penniless girl. Reviewing this misdeed in his maturer years, he blamed it on his sensibilities, of which he had not a jot. Melanie Herbert had been the loveliest vision ever formed by nature, hardly a woman at all, but an angel come to earth to wreak havoc among mankind, and her major havoc had been wrought on his own ambitions. A younger son, his duty was to marry a fortune, but at the crucial period of his life when the choice was to be made, he fell in love. Over the decades he had worked hard to make up for this one lapse, turning his small estate, New Moon, into a fairly thriving and profitable one. But he was not a rich man, and not a happy one.

Melanie's beauty faded fast; her ripe charms reached their apogee when she was twenty-one and decayed rather swiftly. The vacant blue eyes which seemed at eighteen to hold promise of bliss held, at twenty-eight, no more than regret. She was pleasingly plump at twenty-five, stout at thirty, and fat at thirty-five. The charming innocence of eighteen stood revealed in later years as ignorance, and the sweet compliance of temperament as sloth.

At forty-five, Sir Gerald found himself hobbled with a fat, stupid, lazy spouse whose only strength was her constitution. She was as healthy as a horse. She hadn't even given her husband a son, but a daughter who bid fair at seventeen to become a replica of herself. Sir Gerald marshaled his resources and determined to wrest from the wreck of his life some profit. Sara, his daughter, had all the physical attractions that had been her mother's. This beautiful bloom was cultivated, nurtured, and tended with all the care given a rare orchid. Her manners were groomed to please the highest-ranking suitors; her face and form were tended with oils and exercise respectively, for no excess of fat must be allowed to build up on that celestial body till she was profitably disposed of in marriage. It was fairly well forgotten that under those golden curls there was a brain that might also have welcomed a little nourishment. No matter weightier than the weather was ever discussed with Sara, for fear of bringing a wrinkle to her perfect brow or a crowsfoot to the corner of that incomparable eye.

But Fate had a cruel trick in store for Sir Gerald. In that same autumn before he planned to present Sara to society, he was stricken down with a heart seizure and died, without having a chance to give his wife instructions as to how to dispose of their daughter. Lady Monteith was left a widow with no more notion of how to keep house than her beautiful and near-witless daughter. Clearly they would sink into disaster if they didn't find a new protector.

Indeed, the idea of getting along without a man in the house to look after them frightened them both out of their wits. Who would speak to bailiffs and butlers, who would give them their allowance? Who would tell them whether they could have a new gown, and advise them as to whether the sofa wanted upholstering and about the dozens of other matters that were as far beyond their own ken as the stock market? Life would surely become a series of calamities. Lady Monteith had neither the energy nor the inclination, nor any longer the looks to find another husband herself, but it eventually dawned on her, at about the time the period of six months' deep mourning was up, that every gentleman they met on the street turned to stare at Sara. There seemed always to be a man there to help them out of their various difficulties, and within another month this needle-witted woman tumbled to it that it was Sara's beauty that was the cause of attraction. Before too long she put two and two together and calculated that it was Sara and not herself who would find them a protector.

She took no action to bring any union about, but this soon proved unnecessary. Sir Gerald's sister descended on them that fall for a visit, and from then on all she had to do was say, 'Yes indeed, Martha. The very thing.' It was almost as good, or as bad, as having Gerald back with them.

Martha was a spinster, not of the meek, submissive, and impoverished sort, but having a great deal of money in her own right. This was inherited from an uncle who had never seen her, and therefore had no cause to hate her. She devoted her life to helping those relatives whom she imagined to be in need of her services. A tall, sharp-nosed, dark-eyed woman whose face was often likened to a hatchet, she ruled her relatives with an iron hand. She had taken on her sister's daughter three years previously when she was orphaned, and Miss Watters had been brought along to New Moon with her, as she was not the sort of girl one dared leave alone. Not that she was bad or wild, but she had a mind of her own, which was a good deal worse in Miss Monteith's view. Neither was Lillian an ill-favored girl—she was fairly attractive in appearance —and Martha could have got her married off years ago if only she did as she was told. But without ever giving the least appearance of pertness or disobedience, Lillian managed to go pretty well her own way. Martha didn't know whether she loved her or hated her, but she knew she had met her match.

Lady Monteith was a different matter. She'd get her and her daughter settled up in the twinkling of an eye, and go back to Barnsley in Yorkshire and continue to pursue Mr. Thorstein for Lillian. "Now, Melanie, what we must do is find a good match for your daughter," she decreed within a quarter of an hour of her arrival at New Moon.

"Yes indeed, Martha, just what I thought myself."

"Who have you in mind?"

"I'm sure any of the gentlemen in the neighorhood would be happy to have her. They all dangle after her in the most marked way when we go to the village."

"I don't like the sound of that! She'll soon be known as a flirt if she isn't already. Let us have the names and the circumstances of them."

"There is Harvey Osmond, so very dashing and handsome. He is always trying to set up a flirtation with Sara."

"What are his circumstances?"

"He's ever so handsome, always happy to carry a parcel or open a door or hold the horses."

"Peagoose! Who is he?"

"He is Squire Osmond's son. They have seven sons. Such a fine family as they are!"

"And Harvey is the eldest?"

"No, no. He is the youngest."

Miss Monteith stared at her sister-in-law. "The *youngest?* Melanie Monteith, you're a fool. What good is a youngest son to us? Not a square foot of ground to call his own, I daresay, and no prospects."

"His papa is trying to get him a position with some Member of Parliament—something of the sort. He is very clever, they say, though he didn't go up to university. The youngest, you know . . ."

"Do you wish to see your only daughter marry a clerk? Your wits have gone begging, woman," Martha snapped.

Melanie blinked her blue eyes twice slowly and smoothed a wrinkle on her gown. After a deal of cogitating she added, "There is Lord Ericson, but he, you know, is married."

"*He* will clearly do us a lot of good! Who else have you in mind?"

At the moment, Melanie hadn't a thing in her mind but a glass of ratafia, but she was just a little intimidated by Miss Monteith, who was so very like Gerald, so she bestirred herself to answer. "Any of the local beaux will be glad to have her. There will be no problem to finding her a husband now that we are out of mourning."

"Who lives in the fine place—I think it was an abbey—I passed two or three miles down the road? Big wrought-iron gates with a swan worked into them?"

"Saint Christopher's Abbey," Melanie told her.

"Who lives at St. Christopher's Abbey?" Martha asked, reining in her temper.

"A man called Anthony Fellows lives there."

"Has he a son who is not taken yet?"

"No, indeed, he has no son at all. He is a bachelor."

Martha could scarcely credit her ears. The next-door neighbor a bachelor of apparent affluence, and the ninny-hammer had never thought to consider him. His age, temperament, preference for a wife with a brain in her head—all were details. "He'll do, then."

"Gerald never liked him."

"It will no doubt come as news to you, Melanie, but Gerald is dead. Dead and buried this twelvemonth. His plan of presenting Sara in London is gone with the wind; there isn't money enough for that with the cost of settling the mortgage, and don't think *I* mean to do it for you, for I don't."

This was a great injustice. Melanie had never given the matter much thought, save to sigh with relief that she would not have to go to London herself after Gerald passed away. A tear oozed out of her big eyes, not at the mention of her husband's death, but at the sharp tone. She hated to be shouted at.

Unmoved, Martha forged on. "Tell me about this Fellows. Well-to-do, I take it from the looks of the place?"

"Yes, very well off. He always seems to have money for everything."

"How large is the estate?"

"Very large." There was clearly no point in expecting a figure from this near-moron and Martha knew it, but she tried for a few more rough details that even Melanie might possibly know. "He has a good character?"

"Very good. No one ever says a word against him."

It was a mere detail, but Martha decided to ask it. "What of his person—his age, appearance?"

"He's youngish," Melanie said with a great yawn only partially concealed behind her pudgy hand.

Martha was forty and Melanie not far behind her. They both considered themselves youngish, and Martha, while she had no great objection to a gentleman in his forties, was curious enough to inquire more closely. "About our age?"

"Younger."

"How young? Old enough to marry?"

"Oh my, yes, not that young, though he isn't much interested in girls. He is about thirty."

Miss Monteith would have preferred a slightly older gentleman. Thirty sounded young enough still to have a wild oat or so in him, and she was interested in propriety. "Well, I hope he is a good, solid, sensible sort of a man."

"Very sensible. Quite serious."

Coming from Melanie, it was a virtually useless statement. Unless he were a raving lunatic he would seem sensible to her. But Martha had heard enough. The very gentleman for Sara had been sitting under her nose forever, and she had done nothing to nab him. It was vexing in the extreme to have had this trip for nothing just when Mr. Thorstein was on the verge of offering for Lillian. He was in the line of manufacturing, unfortunately, but very well to do, and he spoke of selling out and moving to his estate very soon. In the interim, Martha had access to woolen goods at a very good price—the usual price being a meal. He came to dinner as often as he was asked, and never empty-handed.

"We will call on Mr. Fellows tomorrow," Miss Monteith announced, and rose. "I am going to my room now. I keep country hours."

"So do we," Melanie said, happy at this coincidence. She considered it in no other light. One or the other of them having to shift her life habits about did not occur to her.

"Dinner at five," Martha added.

"That's when we eat too," Melanie said, smiling, and poured herself a glass of ratafia as soon as she was left alone.

Sara Monteith and Lillian Watters had been allowed to stray into the garden to become acquainted, for Martha did not consider it any of the younger girl's business what man should be chosen for her to marry. Though the garden was past its prime, it being the very end of September, a few roses and other flowers were to be seen, forming a pretty background for the girls. From a little distance, they both looked young and pretty and amused at each other's company, but a closer inspection would have revealed an inequality in both appearance and amusement.

Miss Monteith had all the advantages. She was the more attractive in appearance and was certainly more amused than her less well-endowed cousin, for it took very little to entertain her. She was content to sit gazing at a flower or a canary for half an hour at a stretch, and a person of very little conversation could hold her captivated endlessly. In fact, she preferred people who didn't talk too much to those who asked hard questions.

She liked Cousin Lillian, although at first glance she had been a little frightened of her. She was old, for one thing—even older than twenty, and therefore an old maid. It always made her nervous, to see nature go so wrong and leave a poor woman with no man to cling to. Then too she had those sharp black eyes that looked as though they knew things. She was afraid Cousin Lillian would be the kind of lady who asked her what books she liked, and whether she played whist, and even what she thought about Napoleon and Wellington or some of those soldiers who were always fighting wars in countries with funny names. The war had been over since June, but Sara had not yet discovered it. She was very happy to live in England where there were no wars, and never had been as far as she knew.

But her cousin had only asked one or two questions, and as soon as she had told her how much she enjoyed reading *Peter Pepper's Perfect Day*, she hadn't bothered her with any more talk of a hard kind. She had read *Peter Pepper's Perfect Day* six times—once a year ever since she was eleven—and intended to plow through it again before Christmas. It was the best book ever written, and she often wished *she* could have such a perfect day. So clever the way the writer could think of hundreds of words all starting with a P. "Peter put pepper on his potato," and "Peter played a pipe," and "Peter pelted pips at people"—dozens of P's on every single page. There was never another book like it. After she had told Cousin Lillian all about the book and offered to lend it to her, she had become very nice indeed, and for the past ten minutes they had been getting acquainted by silently looking at the leaves together and smiling.

"The lovely leaves look languid," Miss Watters said after a long pause.

"Yes, they do," Sara agreed, though she was not quite sure what languid meant.

"And the grass is growing greatly," Lillian added a long minute later.

"Yes, it is," Sara answered. Then she frowned. There was something odd in this conversation, but she couldn't quite put her finger on it. "It's the rain that makes it grow," she told Lillian, for she didn't wish to appear stupid. They both looked at the grass a while longer, then Miss Watters began to move about from boredom.

"Lounging ladies lack liveliness," she said firmly, and rose. "Will you show me your garden, Cousin?"

Another frown creased Sara's brow. Since her papa was no longer there to chide her for the habit, she was frowning two or three times a week. "That rhymes," she said, having solved the mystery of her cousin's talk at last.

"Not quite, but you're on the track," Lillian replied, and gave Sara a hand to get up from the bench.

"Just like Peter Pepper! Cousin, have you read a book too?" she demanded.

"I have read three or four," Lillian told her, "but I

have never read one six times, so you needn't fear I'll outpace you."

"I wish you will tell me their names, for they sound just the sort I will love. 'Lazy ladies lack lounging'—how clever."

Lillian opened her mouth to make a correction, but thought better of it. "How vexing! I didn't bring them with me for you to read, when you have been kind enough to loan me Peter Pepper."

"Oh, that's all right. I daresay we shan't have time to read anyway, now that you are here. Aunt Martha plans to marry me, you know."

Lillian's dark eyes filled with laughter, but alas, there was no one to share the joke with. "Do you mean to have her?" she quizzed.

"Oh yes, as long as she finds me a legible *partie*, I shall be satisfied, for I don't want to be a spinster like her and you."

"A heavy reader like yourself will certainly want a *legible* gentleman," Lillian returned, and found occasion to blow her nose immediately and to go to her room very shortly afterward, to dissolve in mirth on her bed.

## 2

THE sole interest at dinner was the food, for there was nothing that could be called conversation at the table. Martha outlined her plans for calling at St. Christopher's Abbey, and neither Melanie nor Sara made any objection. If Mr. Fellows should find it odd that his next-door neighbors suddenly came to call after not doing so for twenty years, it was not thought worth a mention. Lillian did say that a country gentleman was not particularly likely to be home to greet callers on a busy weekday morning, but her aunt was a step ahead of her. She had sent over a note, in Lady Monteith's name, expressing their intention.

After dinner, Martha retired early and took Lillian upstairs with her to outline to her what she had discovered of Mr. Fellows, ending up with, "And I see you have discovered your cousins are fools, Lillian, but that is no reason you must make it obvious to Mr. Fellows. Pray keep your sharp tongue between your teeth, and don't be clever or satirical."

"Why Auntie, I am hurt! You never accused me of it before, only of trying to be. I wouldn't do a thing to turn such a legible *partie* off from Cousin Sara."

Her aunt regarded her through narrowed eyes. "You are not enunciating properly. Young ladies nowadays think it smart to mumble."

"You know well enough we haven't a word to say for ourselves, and try to hide the dearth of our conversation with a mumble."

"Yes . . . well, pray don't mumble before Mr. Fellows. It will be up to us to do the talking, to try to conceal their total ignorance, and it must be done discreetly. No flirting with him."

"How should it be possible for us two spinsters to set up a flirtation, at our age?" Lillian laughed and gave her fusty old aunt a hug.

"No manners!" Martha grouched, not deceiving her niece in the least that she disliked such treatment.

"Manners enough that I shan't flirt with Mr. Fellows. Unless he should prove to be handsome, of course."

Martha gave up and decided that if worse came to worst, Lillian should marry Fellows and be put in charge of finding Sara a different husband.

The four ladies called on Mr. Fellows early the next morning. Martha was busy pointing out the advantages of his estate as they went along: stonework in good repair, at least twenty bedrooms in that house if she knew anything, and the shrubberies neatly trimmed. She was similarly pleased with the interior of her niece's future home. Good taste was displayed in the find old furnishings and, of far more importance in her view, there was no dust or dirt in evidence, but a pleasing smell of beeswax and turpentine hanging on the air, indicating the work of a well-ordered staff.

Martha was, of course, interested to see the groom above all, and to determine that he didn't wear high shirt-points or use a scent. His plain blue jacket proved acceptable, and his faun trousers and Hessians received an approving nod, on account of their not being buckskins and topboots in which to receive a visit from ladies. Her hypercritical eyes scarcely saw that he was a well-set-up gentleman with a passing handsome face. He was either too polite or lacking in interest to inquire the reason for the visit, but accepted it as though it were a commonplace.

For ten minutes the five sat conversing about the weather and straightening out the relationship in which the four visitors stood to each other. Lillian found it odd that the gentleman's eyes should not more often stray to Sara, she was so exquisitely beautiful; and as she had not yet said more than good day, he could not know she was a fool. But he paid neither young girl any special heed.

It became clear that his mind was greatly occupied

with some other matter than his callers, and Mr. Fellows, at last allowed his preoccupation to come out. "I have been asked to stand for Parliament," he said.

"Fancy that!" Lady Monteith rhapsodized.

"What party?" Martha rapped out suspiciously.

"Oh, for the Whigs," he said, on the defense. Sir Gerald had been a Tory, a cause of enmity between them when he himself had switched a few years ago. Martha too had once been a Tory, but she never liked to agree with her family on anything, and for that and other reasons had become a Whig within the recent past. She smiled in satisfaction at his answer, not that it was a matter of great importance one way or the other.

Mr. Fellows then launched into a political monologue, secure that he was among friends. "After looking into the matter, I concluded the country's only hope of salvation lies with the Whigs. As Lord Allingham was saying the other night, till we drive those reactionary Tories from the seats of power, there is no hope for England. It was Lord Allingham who convinced me it was my duty to run. A man has a duty beyond his own back yard. He and Basingstoke between them talked me into it, that is to say, for certainly Mr. Basingstoke is a very well-educated gentleman, even though he hasn't a title."

"Being educated surely is part and parcel of being a gentleman," Martha pointed out. Even a prospective groom was subject to her little moralizings.

"Yes," Mr. Fellows agreed, very briefly for him, and he looked uncomfortable.

"It is not time for a general election, is it?" Lillian asked. She did not happen to be keenly interested in politics, but could not believe a general election had been called without her having heard of it.

"No, it is only a by-election. Our incumbent, a Tory, died; the Rt. Honorable James Farrington passed away a fortnight ago. You would have heard of it, Lady Monteith." He turned to his neighbor.

"I don't believe I did," she answered, and wondered that he didn't offer them a glass of wine or a cup of tea. However, this lapse on the host's part was soon remedied, and with a plateful of biscuits and a glass of wine before her, Lady Monteith retired from the conversation.

"So you will be busy politicking the next month or so?" Martha questioned, wondering if this would interfere with his wooing of Sara, at whom he had scarcely bothered to glance the past while.

"Lord Allingham is giving me a hand with my campaign. A Mr. Hudson is being sent down from London to manage it. He is very influential in the party, though not actually an elected member. He is a sort of party manager —a whip, Allingham called him. Basingstoke was saying he got our man in in some little borough or other—I forget the name—that was always Tory before. They always send a Tory here from Crockett too, but Hudson will whip me in. There is a wind of change in the country, I think, after the war, with the veterans coming back and being treated like dogs. The next general election may see a changeover from the repressive party that has been riding roughshod over this country the last years."

"Back to the days of Fox, eh, Mr. Fellows?" Martha said with a rare polite interest. "That's the spirit."

"Aye, Lord Allingham was mentioning something about Fox the other evening. What an orator the man was! He could talk for hours and sway the entire Parliament. I daresay he was a well-educated gentleman."

"What are the issues on which you will fight the

campaign?" Martha asked. She would have preferred to speak of balls and drives and pleasure outings, but Mr. Fellows seemed to be bent on business.

He looked a little startled. "Why, against the repressive and reactionary measures of the Tories," he said.

"Yes, but what measures?"

"Oh, you ladies are not interested in politics, I daresay," he told her with condescension. "Basingstoke said something about getting some road or other surfaced, and a bridge over the Severn River. It is very awkward not having a bridge to Chepstow, the town just north of us across the river. There is only that blasted barge now, or driving ten miles to take the Lydney Bridge. It is certainly a disgrace that we have no bridge at Crockett."

"Would it not be the Tory member, the member of the party in power, who could deliver that?" Lillian inquired.

She was not surprised at his answer, for she had been beginning to suspect it was the repressive Tories who had been depriving them of it all these years. "The Tories, you know, always repress any liberal policy that will help the common people," she was told. "Much they care in London that we have to trust our nags to Jed Harper's old barge to get to Chepstow, or ride the ten miles to Lydney. If elected, I will certainly do all within my power to get a bridge for the town of Crockett."

"If the Tory member who just died couldn't get it, Mr. Fellows, how would you go about it?" Martha asked.

"I would do all in my power to get it. Basingstoke says he will speak to Hudson and see if something can't be done about it. Well, it seems to me you ladies are more interested in politics than most females, and as you are all Whigs, I hope you will put in a good word for me, if the opportunity should arise."

Lillian found herself waiting to hear Lord Allingham's views on women and politics, but they were not offered. Martha, no slouch in summing up the host, decided he was not yet in love with Sara, and to hasten the affair along she said, "We will be happy to do what we can to help you, Mr. Fellows. Be sure to give us a call if you need us. Writing letters or doing any little jobs of a routine sort that might eat up your valuable time will be a pleasure for us. We are all interested in seeing the Whigs win."

Lady Monteith, whose husband hated the Whigs nearly as much as he hated the French, nodded her head in approval. She found the whole conversation incomprehensible, as did her beautiful daughter.

"What is a Whig?" Sara asked.

"He is a man who is liberal-minded," Mr. Fellows told her, which did nothing to enlighten her. She wanted to inquire what was liberal-minded, and what was an election, but her aunt was frowning at her, so she desisted. It sounded interesting if it meant a bridge to Chepstow, for the shops there were much larger and better than at Crockett.

"I'm glad you didn't ask me what is a Tory!" Mr. Fellows proclaimed—meaning, of course, why don't you?

"What is your definition of a Tory?" Lillian asked, curious to hear Lord Allingham's view.

"A Tory is a Conservative. He would conserve power and money to himself, principles to the Whigs, and hard work and poverty to the people," he said with a satisfied smile.

"Very good, Mr. Fellows," Martha congratulated him.

"Mr. Basingstoke goes on to suggest that a Tory is a man who has not yet seen the light and become a Whig, but Allingham tells me not to say so, for though Fox came to us from the Tory camp, Castlereagh went the other way, from Whig to Tory. Indeed, they all switch about a good deal. My father was a Tory and so was I myself before I saw the light, but I never *ran* as a Tory. Basingstoke says that is in my favor—not to have shown my colors before. He is longheaded as may be, Basingstoke. He went to Oxford and took a degree."

There seemed little hope of romance from a gentleman whose head was so obviously full of politics and his patrons, so the ladies took their leave, urging him half a dozen times to call on them at New Moon.

"I will certainly avail myself of your kind offer, ladies," he said, and escorted them to the door. Already a politician, he had a smile for them all, and at the end a special glance in recognition of Sara's beauty. He blinked at her and then looked in admiration for a full thirty seconds. It was odd it had taken him so long to recognize her as an Incomparable, but certain among the ladies already doubted he was a needle-witted man, and thought that with a nudge he might find himself in love with Sara.

They drove home to consider further plans to entrap him. It was the elder Miss Monteith who hit on the idea of taking an active part in the campaign. They would hold a tea party to help him along, and invite all the local ladies whose husbands, sons or brothers had a vote and any of the gentlemen who were free to attend. Mr. Fellows would be present to tell them about the repression of the Tories, and to give them a definition of just what a Whig was anyway. Martha declared that his being a bachelor was bound to bring out every mother with a daughter to dispose of, and that his engagement to Sara must not be announced till after he was elected. Lillian did not feel this would present any pressing problem, but like a dutiful niece she kept her opinion to herself and let on she had found him "conversable," which was the strange epithet Martha came up with to describe his speeches.

*3*

~~~~~~~~~~~~~~~~~~~~~~~~~~~~~~~~~~~~~~~~~~~~~~~~~~~~~~

THE household at New Moon was delighted to receive an invitation to dinner at St. Christopher's Abbey the very next day. It was accepted eagerly, the party to meet at six. To sustain themselves for what promised to be a late dinner, they had tea late and set out shortly after 5:30. They assumed it was to be a regular dinner party, and Martha and Lillian were looking forward to meeting Lord Allingham and Mr. Basingstoke among the required extra gentlemen. Certainly Lady Monteith hadn't an idea who might be on visiting terms with her next-door neighbor. But when they were shown into his saloon, there was only one other gentleman present, and he was a stranger to them all.

Mr. Hudson was first taken to be an elderly gentleman, for he had gray wings at the temples of his dark hair, but upon closer inspection he was seen to be neither lined nor hagged, and his age was set as being no more than in the early thirties. It was clear at a glance he was no country squire. The sleek barbering of his hair, the lines of his black jacket and his easy manners proclaimed a metropolitan gentleman of fashion. The elder Miss Monteith quickly pegged him as a "smart" or "swell," while Miss Watters noted with interest that there was present on his countenance a quick change of expression, a sensitiveness, an intelligence that made her hope the conversation under Mr. Fellows's roof might be improved from her last visit. Sara thought he looked divinely handsome but was quite likely of that breed that asked hard questions.

They were all made acquainted, and Sara didn't know whether she was gratified or terrified when Mr. Hudson appeared at some little pains to gain a seat beside her. His first question did not prove impossible of replying to with dignity. She knew very well she lived at New Moon, and how far away it was. She was able to verify such details as her father's death a year previously and her aunt and cousin visiting them from Yorkshire without wrinkling her brow. She was less easy when he inquired what she felt Mr. Fellows's chances to be in the election, but she said at least that she hoped he would win, for she did want to see a bridge between Crockett and Chepstow, and the Tories wouldn't let them have one. She was truly at a loss when he asked whether all the girls at Crockett were as pretty as herself, but she knew it for a compliment, and colored up so prettily that Mr. Hudson accepted a second glass of sherry and leaned back in her chair with satisfaction to pass the time till dinner in her company.

This left Mr. Fellows to entertain the three other ladies, and he did so by telling them that Mr. Hudson was going to be an excellent whipper-in. "He is very strict, mind you," he told them. "We want to run a good, clean campaign. No smear tactics. It will be fought on principles and issues."

Indeed, Mr. Hudson's appearance gave no reason to doubt this. With his dignified gray hair, his face of a noble cast, and his serious expression, he looked a perfect judge. How should they know that he was teasing the life out of Sara, and telling her that when she walked through the door he had thought she was an angel come to earth to guide Fellows to victory? They took her squirming embarrassment to be the result of hard questions—those of them who paid any attention at all to her.

But Mr. Fellows was still Martha's first priority, and she turned to speak to him. "It may begin that way," she said, "but it has been my experience in the past that sooner or later you will both end up sinking into *argumentum ad hominem* tactics. It happened in the West Riding at the last election. They accused our Whig of being an atheist."

Mr. Fellows looked aghast. He had never expected such a low trick from a female as spouting Latin at him. His gentlemen acquaintances he knew to be sadly addicted to this vice, especially those who had been to university. He never had himself. He had twice applied to Oxford and been twice rejected as inadequately prepared, despite years of tutoring and study. He felt this deficiency of formal education in his background very strongly. It was his ardent desire to be taken for an Oxford man, and to this end he introduced every break-teeth word he knew into his discourse, and even had a dozen Latin quotations ready to use, but *argumentum ad hominem* was not one of them. He was lost.

"Do you think so?" he asked, hoping for enlightenment.

"It always happens," Miss Monteith replied unhelpfully.

He looked nervously across the room to his manager. There was a fellow who would know exactly what she was talking about. "What do you have to say to this, Mr. Hudson?" he asked.

Mr. Hudson looked up and asked for the question again. He had spent a wearying afternoon with his new acquaintance, and after having mentioned that money was a *sine qua non* to winning, and having had to explain this, he deduced the problem as soon as he heard the question.

"I hope you may be wrong, Miss Monteith," he said. "I hope it does not come down to an *ad hominem* campaign—our two candidates making charges of a personal and abusive nature against each other. We hope to keep the tone higher than that, but should that be the case, I don't think we need fear. Mr. Fellows has nothing to hide. He has never done anything. Anything wrong I mean," he added quickly, seeing what had accidentally slipped out. It was in fact a pity Mr. Fellows had never done anything right either—never done a single thing for the community at large. Never headed a single committee or set up a petition or even put his signature to one. He feared that despite Mr. Fellows's being one of the best-off people in the neighborhood, he had kept very much to himself and did not have a large circle of friends and supporters to fall back on. It seemed hard that the party had saddled him with such an unpopular man in this difficult riding.

He forsaw many difficulties in putting this handsome dummy up for election, but overcoming difficulties was his job, so he was not despondent about pulling the thing off. He had hoped to get down to business tonight with Basingstoke and Allingham and give Fellows a good briefing—of which he clearly stood in need—and so had welcomed the idea of a dinner party where he could meet some local worthies and feel them out on the issues. Instead, the party consisted of themselves and four females. Not one vote in the party, except for Fellows himself. He didn't know what Fellows was about to waste a whole evening, but once he was fairly caught in the toils, it was too late to do anything, and Hudson hoped to pass the time with a little flirtation with the fair charmer on his left. She was a stunning-looking creature, but seemed stunned as well, alas. One could admire a pretty doll for only so long, and he had about had his fill of looking.

"We certainly need not fear an *ad hominem* campaign," Mr. Fellows assured them all, storing up the phrase eagerly to add to his list. "If Alistair sinks to that, people are bound to hear about his prison record."

Mr. Hudson started from his seat in surprise and delight. For hours together that afternoon he had been trying to discover something about Alistair, the Conservative candidate, and had gained nothing but that he was a bruising rider to hounds and kept a good cellar. He had been heartily wishing it were Alistair he had been running. And now, out of the blue, to hear the man had a prison record. It was manna from heaven.

"You told me nothing about that, Mr. Fellows! What is his record?"

"Why, it was young Alistair who was on the committee to look into conditions at Dartmoor, that prison they set up at Prince Town for the French captives from the war, and he made a botch of it. They said—Allingham mentioned it—that it took them so long to look into it the war was over before they sent their report, and then there was nothing in it."

Hudson stared at him. "You mean he *worked* on a commission to look into prison conditions? *That* is his prison record?"

"Certainly he did, and made a botch of it. They only dragged it out so long to line their pockets. The Tories are all alike, grabbing every cent they can get their hands on. His prison record is nothing to be proud of."

"I see," Mr. Hudson said weakly, and didn't know whether to laugh or cry. "I had hoped you meant he had been to prison himself."

"What, an *Alistair* in prison?" Fellows asked, shocked. "Gracious me, no! They are an excellent old family. We have known them forever."

"That's too bad," Mr. Hudson said.

"You would not have used the fact, Mr. Hudson?" Lillian asked. "You said you did not intend to make it that sort of a campaign. No dragging up disgraceful conduct on either side. No *ad hominem* arguments."

"A prison record would be something quite different.

It is actually illegal for a man with a prison record—for certain crimes, that is—to run for Parliament at all. Certainly for such behavior as that I would feel justified to raise the question of personal conduct."

"Yes, I suppose you are right," she allowed.

Mr. Hudson, his attention now directed at Miss Watters, looked at her more closely than he had done before. Not a beautiful girl; brown hair, very dark eyes—her finest feature. A little thinner than he liked, but not a bad-looking girl at all.

"I never cared for homonyms myself," Sara said to him in a consoling fashion.

"Did you not?" he asked, perplexed. He thought he must have missed some intervening statement on her part. She had a low-pitched voice that was pleasing to him, but required sharp listening.

The two groups fell into separate discourse till dinner was called. Mr. Fellows made some effort to balance his lopsided party, putting Mr. Hudson at its foot, with one young lady and one aunt along either side of the board. Liking Sara's admiring and undemanding conversation, he kept her for himself and placed Miss Watters on Hudson's left. This was the first chance either had to form any clear idea of the other. Hudson repeated a few of his questions already posed to Sara to Miss Watters; then he asked her one that would have terrified her cousin. Did she have any experience at all in politics?

"Only in Yorkshire, and there you know the only issue in the campaign was the Luddites. The country at large may be concerned about other things, but at Barnsley the campaign was fought over the textile industry and the efforts of the manufacturers to introduce machines that will throw many people out of work. Those who do work find it extremely degrading and mechanical, sitting at a machine all day long. And of course the product turned out is grossly inferior."

"Still, I think it foolish the way the Luddites set about righting what is certainly a grave wrong—forming groups to smash the machines. There must be a more sensible way to solve the matter. Who is this Captain Ludd who has organized the workers? Is he an actual person?"

"He is a general now, if you please—General Ned Ludd. Well, he *is* a real person, but a sort of village idiot from Leicestershire. He was chasing some children who were tormenting him one day, and followed them into their home, where they managed to hide from him. He vented his anger on their parents' frames, and so now whenever machinery is destroyed, it is said to be done by General Ludd, no matter who actually did it. It pre- serves anonymity for the workers."

"Violence is no answer. It begets more violence, and we'll end up with a civil war on our hands."

"Try if you can convince the government of it in London. When the workers were prevented by law from setting up a trade union, they formed an 'Institution,' using the pretext of its being a sick club to tend to the needs of members out of work through illness. The Insti- tution went to London to present its case to the Parlia- mentary Committee on the Woolen Trade, and the members were treated little better than criminals. They had some good ideas, too, such as a tax on woolen goods to help tide the unemployed workers over till they could find some other work. And even when frameworkers got a weak bill through the Commons, it was thrown out by the Lords. No alternative was left to them but violence."

"That's the Tories for you."

"Yes. With the mill-owners holding the majority of the votes, a Tory member was returned and the rioting was pretty-well squelched by the army, but it was an infamous thing. It turned many people into Whigs, my aunt and myself included. But we are not informed Whigs; it is a reaction against the Tories rather. All this business will have little influence on the election here, I suppose. What do you see as the issues in this by-election?"

"We'll make it local issues," he said.

"*Make* it? But surely there are real issues that ought to be discussed. You can't just *make* issues."

"Concentrate on local issues, I mean. People are interested in what goes on in their own back yards more than in what is going on in the country as a whole. Well, you just proved it, didn't you, by saying your election was fought on the issue of the Luddite riots? This is a farming community; the Luddites will not interest them. It is the damned—excuse me—the price of corn that will be one issue certainly."

"And a poor one for you! The farmers are all in favor of the Corn Laws the Tory government passed. It is good for their pockets, guaranteeing them ten shillings a bushel."

"I am aware of it, and foresee the need of another issue as well."

"What does Mr. Fellows suggest?" she asked, wondering if Mr. Hudson had had more luck talking to him than they had themselves."

"He mentions the war quite often, but I see no gain to be got from that. It's over. Of course there are the veterans who are not treated well. Very likely that's what he meant."

She gave him a commiserating smile that implied she

understood his predicament in trying to get a man of such small understanding elected. "How does it come Mr. Fellows was chosen to run?" she asked.

"It was Lord Allingham's suggestion. He is influential in these parts. They had difficulty in getting a local man to run, for the riding has been Tory for years. We didn't like to waste a good man—that is, a man who might have a better chance of winning a seat elsewhere, a man who is a little known nationally. Fellows is a good man. We feel ourselves fortunate that he agreed to stand."

Lillian regarded him closely but could see no irony or humor in his foolish statement. She deduced that Mr. Hudson was either a humbug or a fool, although he did not speak like a fool. "A good deal must depend on Mr. Alistair. If he is a strong candidate, you will have a hard task on your hands."

"Yes, I'm eager to meet Mr. Alistair."

The ladies retired to the saloon and the gentlemen soon joined them. On this occasion Mr. Hudson sought out a seat beside Miss Watters. She had been waiting with some eagerness to see where he chose to place himself, and was aware of a slight flutter in her breast when he came toward her without even a glance at Sara. She was soon enlightened as to the unflattering nature of his attention: he wished to ask her to address a batch of envelopes for him and to send out some circulars he was having printed up outlining Mr. Fellows's imaginary qualities as a good Member of Parliament. She was not entirely displeased with him, however, when he said with a warm smile that he looked forward to the pleasure of delivering the material in person and learning more from her of conditions in the West Riding.

The matter settled, they both turned to hear Mr. Fellows expounding to Sara his views of the repressive and reactionary Tories.

"What do they repress?" she asked, batting her long lashes at him.

"Everything," he answered comprehensively.

"Dear me, that is very bad of them," she said. "And what do they react against?"

"Us Whigs, mostly," he told her with a knowing smile.

"Fancy that nice Mr. Alistair being such a reactor. I wouldn't have expected it of him."

"He is of very good family and an excellent man in other ways. But they sent him off to Cambridge, you know. He was never at Oxford at all, and very likely that's why he became a Tory."

"Papa was used to say he'd make some girl a fine husband, and I think he meant me. But of course Papa was a Tory himself. He called Lord Allingham 'a dashed Whig aristocrat.' He always reacted against everything too, my papa—kittens and cream buns and going to the village. I wish he had been a Whig."

"He would have, had he lived, Miss Monteith, depend on it. Well, very likely he has become one in heaven, for you may be sure there are no Tories there. Basingstoke was saying only t'other day a Tory is a Whig who has not yet seen the light, and if your papa had lived to see the light he would have become a Whig, as I did, and as I mean to see the whole riding do."

"What riding?"

"Our riding!" he answered.

"Oh." In her head she pictured a bunch of horsemen riding along, and frowned.

They continued to converse in this manner for fifteen minutes, each gaining a very good idea of the other's limitations. For his part, Mr. Hudson felt his heart sink when he saw what a paucity of material he had to make look wise and sensible.

The elderly ladies, especially Miss Monteith, were happy to see Sara get on so famously with Mr. Fellows, and thought it as good as a proposal when he said he would come with Mr. Hudson tomorrow to deliver the envelopes for addressing.

"And to plan the timing of our tea party," Martha added, for this had been one of the major subjects of discussion after dinner. The tea party was to start a wave that would wash Mr. Fellows into power.

"Yes, by Jove, I *do* like a tea party," Mr. Fellows said. "And with so many ladies present it will be a decorous do. That will please you, Mr. Hudson. No *ad hominem* tactics before the ladies, what?"

"*Ad mulierem,* perhaps," Mr. Hudson answered, but received only a blank stare from all his listeners. "It seems an excellent idea," he said, and thought to himself, another afternoon wasted. But no date had been set and he'd get out of it if better things to do occurred to him.

In the carriage on the way home, Aunt Martha ruled the conversation. "Really, I find Mr. Fellows most conversable. A very nice gentleman. And Mr. Hudson too seems to have proper ideas. His gray hair gives him a dignified appearance. He will handle this campaign with propriety; I'm glad to see he has no ideas of blackening his opponent's character or any low tricks of that sort. Indeed they are two fine gentlemen, and if you didn't have Mr. Thorstein on the string, Lillian, I should make a push to attract Mr. Hudson for *you.* But then we actually know nothing of him. A well-cut jacket and a pleasing smile tell nothing."

They told Miss Watters, however, that she found Mr. Hudson a good deal more interesting than the portly Mr. Thorstein, and she looked forward to seeing him the next morning.

Receiving no affirmation of her opinion, Martha went on to make sure Lillian understood her. "Between Mr. Hudson and Mr. Fellows there is no question of superiority. Mr. Fellows is the better man in every way." Aunt Martha, of course, knew better than this, but for purposes of conversation and marriage she subscribed to a mysterious theory by which rich ladies became automatically accomplished and pretty, rich gentlemen well-bred, and titled ones distinguished. Mr. Fellows, with a fortune and an abbey at his back, had taken a leap to conversability. Mr. Hudson, on the other hand, though he had the noble mien of a duke or a judge, wit and intelligence to spare, and manners, had no known worldly goods but the coat on his back, and she soon began discerning a touch of something "low" about him. She would not be more specific, but his being sent to Crockett as a clerk and errand boy for Mr. Fellows—as she conceived his duties —had definitely given him a low air that no manners or tailoring or gray hair could quite conceal. It would take a fortune at least to remove that trace of lowness.

*4*

HAVING wasted a whole precious evening with four unenfranchised ladies, Mr. Hudson was eager to get on with the campaign in the morning. As soon as breakfast was over, he suggested riding over to Lord Allingham's place for a discussion, and Mr. Fellows was all compliance. There was little he would rather do than visit a lord.

"We'll take along the envelopes for the ladies to address, as we'll be passing by New Moon," he said.

"Yes, we'll drop them off along the way to save time," Hudson agreed.

It saved no time, as they were invited in for a cup of coffee, which Mr. Hudson was forced to accept when Fellows expressed so much eagerness. He hoped to spend the time in discovering something of local issues, but the Monteith ladies who lived at Crockett were strangely uninformed. They both welcomed the idea of a bridge, but on other matters they appeared totally ignorant. The other visitors, with obviously a keener interest, were only visitors, and of such short standing that they could tell him nothing. Mr. Hudson fielded questions as to the preferred time for the tea party without being pinned down, and in half an hour got his candidate out the door.

Allingham was only slightly interested in the election. "Crockett never elected a Whig and never will," he told Hudson bluntly, when they had sent Fellows over to the window to peruse some Whig doctrine. "If we had had a top-notch candidate we might have made a decent showing, but no one wants to run here. We have no hope of getting our man in, so we are running Fellows. He has been having some doings with Basingstoke lately; it was Basingstoke's idea to have him stand. He is well inlaid and can bear the expense. He will like the consequence of running."

"It won't add much to his consequence if he gets no more than a handful of votes. You give up too easily, Allingham. Fellows makes the right appearance; he is a good-looking man and a bachelor. I know of nothing against him. I hope I am not down here on a fool's errand."

"I was surprised to hear it was you who was coming. I should have thought Brougham would have more useful work for his party whip. Wasting your time here."

"Things are quiet in London at the moment. My orders were to get him in, and I have been given a full purse to do it—no holds barred. Can I count on your help, and Basingstoke's?"

"Be happy to do what we can, both of us. I wouldn't count too heavily on Basingstoke, though. Not a bright chap. Not bright."

"Not squeamish, I hope?"

"He does pretty well what I tell him."

"Good. Now fill me in on the local issues."

"Just what you'd expect in a farming community—the price of grain, of course. With the farmers all for the Corn Laws, a Whig has no chance, no chance at all."

"Crockett seems a thriving community. The merchants with a vote must nearly equal the farmers; I saw a few small manufactures on the way here. A tanning factory, and as far as that goes, the farmers don't all grow grain. The Corn Laws are no benefit to those who grow other foods. The livestock growers, for instance, can't relish the high cost of grain."

"There's only a handful of them, not enough to counterbalance the corn vote. They like to have their member be of the party in power, too. An opposition member can do little for them."

"I keep hearing something about a bridge to Chepstow. What exactly is the score on that?"

"There used to be one ten years ago and it was washed away and never replaced. The government keeps promis-

ing us one—every election the promise is renewed and
never kept. Well, they know they have this riding sewed
up, don't worry about it. It would be a very good thing
for the townspeople and the farmers, too, to get to their
northern market."

"Tories aren't the only ones who can build bridges."

"They control the purse. I hope you don't expect us
to pay for a bridge out of our own pockets. It would cost
thousands, and the place would still go Tory."

"Would you care to make a small wager, milord?"

"Yes, by God, or better, a large one."

"Shall we say five hundred pounds?"

"Clap hands on a bargain!" Lord Allingham said.

There was nothing further to be gained from a col-
league who considered the election lost before the campaign was begun, so Hudson herded his man back to the
village, there to go into every shop and make a purchase
in order to gain an introduction to the voters. He contrived to make himself agreeable by praising their stores,
their wares, their village, their wives and daughters and
anything else that belonged to them. He soon became
aware that Mr. Fellows was not warmly greeted anywhere.
He was only dimly recognized and kept at a respectful
distance.

"Be a little friendlier if you can, Mr. Fellows," he
advised.

"It don't do to be too friendly with Cits," the man
answered. "They will expect to be first-naming me and
eating at my table if I start that. If you lie down with
dogs, you get fleas."

"They had better be first-naming you and eating at
your table if you wish to win this election, and never mind
the fleas. I shall call you Tony to give them the lead.

You might as well call me Matt, as we are to live in each other's pocket the next month. Now, we are going into this shop here—what is it? A greengrocer—for God's sake buy something."

"Meadows doesn't keep a thing in his shop worth buying. Withered turnips, wilted cabbages and sprouting onions, all at a huge price."

"The best wilted vegetables you have ever seen, Tony. Buy a bushel of each, and don't haggle about the price."

"I have my root cellar full of better stuff than he sells."

"These are for distribution to the needy. Open up that fat purse of yours, if you want to be the Honorable Anthony Fellows, M.P." The lately deceased incumbent of the riding, the Rt. Honorable James Farrington, owed his Honorable to being a Member of the Privy Council, but this detail did not bother Fellows, nor did it bother Hudson much to throw in this unearned perquisite.

A title before his name and letters after it—just like a lord or a university graduate, or both rolled into one inestimable whole. "By Jove," said Fellows, smiling, "I'll do it. Money, eh, Matt? The old *sine qua non's,* as you mentioned t'other day."

"That's the dandy, Tony, and *caveat emptor.*"

"Eh?"

"Let the buyer beware. I mean, don't say anything to offend Mr. Meadows, but the phrase *usually* means . . ." He went on with a little free lesson in Latin for the scholar *manqué.* They bought a great many items at the greengrocer's shop and others, and then went along to the Cat's Paw Inn for lunch and a chat with the proprietor, who had to be introduced to the candidate! At the rather disappointing meal's conclusion, Hudson pushed Tony forward to express his delight to the owner and his intention of returning again very soon.

There was an open stall market in progress, and Hudson walked his candidate along to it, bowing and smiling to everyone they had met that morning and trying to get Tony to do the same. He saw that Mr. Reising, whom the Tories had sent down to get their man in, had beat him to it. The well-set-up young gentleman with him, he assumed, was Alistair. He looked five or six years younger than Tony and nineteen or twenty times as bright. He too was a local citizen, and obviously on the best of terms with everyone. It took a great deal of back-slapping and handshaking on Hudson's part—he a stranger —to give any show at all of Tony's being popular.

He was very happy indeed to see the ladies from New Moon across the way. They had been watching him, a little surprised to see him so much at home in the community he had come to just the day before. His distinguished appearance, heightened by his well-cut jacket and gray hair, stood out in the motley crowd of country folks.

"He gives a good impression, does he not?" Lillian asked her cousin.

"I never saw anything half so handsome," Sara answered.

"It is surprising he knows so many people. He got here only yesterday."

"He has lived here forever, Cousin."

This reply informed Miss Watters that they were discussing two different gentlemen, but at least, she thought, they were looking at the same duo. "Oh, you refer to Mr. Fellows."

"Mr. Fellows? No indeed, I mean Mr. Alistair."

"The Conservative?" Lillian asked with interest.

"No, he's a Tory," Sara told her.

"They mean the same thing, Cousin, as a Whig, you know, is another label for a Liberal. But which is Mr. Alistair?"

"The awfully handsome one in the blue jacket."

Nine-tenths of the gentlemen wore blue jackets, but there weren't many that could be designated as handsome, and by following Sara's intent gaze, Lillian soon picked out Mr. Alistair as being a tall, good-looking blond gentleman, accompanied by an older, gray-haired man to whom the term seedy seemed to apply—not for any dishevelment in his toilette—but owing to an air of dissipation in his face.

"So that's Mr. Alistair. I think he will give Mr. Fellows a good run for his money. He seems popular," Lillian said.

"All the girls are crazy for him," Sarah assured her.

"I meant popular with the townspeople, the farmers—generally popular. He'll get a lot of votes."

"He's looking at us," Sarah said in a low, excited voice.

He was indeed not only looking at them, but walking toward them, and at the same time Mr. Hudson and Mr. Fellows were coming toward them from the opposite direction. The two groups converged at the same time on the four females from New Moon, and while Miss Monteith and Lady Monteith greeted the Whigs, the Tories were greeted by the young ladies. Miss Watters had to admit she was more impressed with Mr. Alistair's charm and wits than she was with Mr. Fellows. He seemed well-spoken, well-mannered, well-informed, well-everything. Her only complaint was in regard to his politics and his mentor, who was introduced as a Mr. Reising from London, Mr. Alistair's campaign manager. Reising's glance more than once went to the group with the elder ladies, and after a few remarks he walked the two steps to join them.

"Well, Mr. Hudson, we meet again," Lillian heard him say. By a few small side-steps she soon edged her way from Sara's side to the other group, watching with interest as Mr. Hudson reached out his hand and gave Mr. Reising's a firm shake, then proceeded to make him known to the ladies as "a friend." She had thought they must be mortal enemies.

"I'll take you this time, Mr. Hudson," Reising said. "But it's no fair fight. I have all the advantages in this riding."

"In the riding, yes, but not in the candidate," Hudson objected. "I have not had the pleasure of your candidate's acquaintance, but I have an excellent man."

"I haven't met yours either. Time we did so, don't you think?"

The omission was taken care of, and within a few minutes Hudson had learned more of interest from his two competitors than he had from any of his cohorts in two days.

"You fight a losing battle," Mr. Alistair told him. "With a promise from my party to build the bridge within eighteen months, I really don't think you stand a chance."

Mr. Hudson heard this awful news without a blink. "They've been promising it for a long time, I understand. Every election the promise is renewed, but never kept."

"It'll be kept this time," Mr. Alistair said very firmly. "When I am elected, I will make it my chief interest to see that Crockett gets its bridge."

"*If* you're elected," Hudson corrected.

"Jolly glad to hear you mean to get that bridge for us," Fellows congratulated his opponent. "Lord Allingham mentioned we might get it, now that an election is upon us."

Mr. Hudson was in despair to see his candidate make such a fool of himself. "Well, we'll believe it when we see it, eh, Tony?"

"If Alistair says he'll get it, we'll get it," Tony confirmed. "But we'll cross that bridge when we get to it, ha ha." As well as his twelve Latin quotations, Fellows had a whole string of clichés at his fingertips. A word triggered a cliché very often, Hudson had observed, and was relieved that this one was not as irrelevant as many others.

"That, of course, must depend on Mr. Alistair's getting elected. Remember you are running against him, Tony," Hudson said.

"That's right. And if I get in we won't see hide nor hair of the bridge, for the repressive Tories run the whole show, you know, and only give the goods to their own ridings."

"I don't think we need worry about your getting in, Mr. Fellows," Reising said, with a glance almost of sympathy at his sworn rival, Hudson. He was a little sorry it was to be such an uneven match; he would have enjoyed a good tight race with Hudson.

Hudson gazed in disbelief at Mr. Fellows. He had never thought he was a clever man, but this was the first evidence he had that he was a complete and utter fool.

"We'll be running along," Reising said. "I see you are going to have your hands full, Mr. Hudson." His eyes flickered in Fellows's direction, and his lips were slightly unsteady.

Then, with bows and farewells, the Tories left.

"My, I wish *I* could vote," Sara said, looking after the wide shoulders of Alistair as he departed.

"Thank you, Miss Monteith," Fellows said. "I appreciate the thought. If wishes were horses, beggars would ride, eh?"

It was not only Sara who was at a loss as to his meaning, if he had any. Mr. Hudson was fagged after the better part of a day with Tony, and thought the undemanding company of the four supporters—and outside of Allingham and Basingstoke they seemed to be the only sure Whigs in the riding—might allow him to lower his vigilance till he had caught his breath.

"We all pitched in and addressed those envelopes this morning," Lillian said to him. "What shall we do with them?"

"What fast workers you are! Thank you very much, I'll pick them up. I begin to think letters might be very useful in this campaign."

Lillian bit her lip to suppress a smile, and as the candidate was telling the other ladies what a tough piece of mutton he had had at the Cat's Paw and warning them away from it, she turned to Mr. Hudson for some private conversation. "Mr. Alistair promises tough competition, I think."

"Oh, I wouldn't say that. Tony is a good chap. A dry wit—his humor is not always appreciated."

She looked at him in astonishment. "Neither is yours in this case. You know he meant no joke. He has a severe case of foot-in-the-mouth and you will have to watch him closely."

"I personally like to see a good, honest man with no tricks about him run for public office. You can trust such a man as that."

"I think Mr. Fellows's tricks were inadvertent, although he played a few nasty ones, and you are generous in your views. But then you mean to run a good, honest, straight-forward campaign, and a little ingenuousness will not go amiss, I suppose."

"You have hit on just the right word. He is ingenuous. An honest, well-meaning, hard-working man."

"I think *you* are working harder than he is, but I hope you are not so ingenuous. It seems to me one of you ought to have your wits about you. Reising has a sly look about him."

"He's as wily as a fox, but he doesn't often beat me, Miss Watters. *One* of us has his wits about him, but thank you for the warning. The envelopes are all addressed, you say?"

"Yes."

"I wonder if you would be interested in another little job for Tony and myself?"

As he had added the magic last word, Miss Watters agreed without even knowing what the job was.

"Tony has bought a great load of stuff today, and we would like you ladies to decide what we should do with it."

"What kind of stuff?" she asked.

"All kinds—vegetables, clothing, various foodstuffs . . ."

"Why did you buy them?"

"To ingratiate the merchants."

"Oh, what an expensive way to do it!"

"It is a sort of charity, and he can well afford it. I have to help Tony prepare for a public meeting at the Veterans' Hall tonight. He and Alistair are to make speeches to the farming community. I have asked the merchants not to deliver the goods till I give them the address, for we don't want it all landing in on us at the abbey. Your aunt will know who could use the things. An orphanage or the local poorhouse, that sort of thing, but distributed as widely as possible."

"Then we must know exactly what you bought, and from which merchants."

"We bought things in every shop—the merchants will tell you what."

"You want us to go into *every shop* in town, you mean, and find out what you bought, and decide where it is to be taken?"

"If it isn't too great an imposition. I wouldn't ask it if your aunt had not so kindly offered to help us in any way she could. And really, I come to feel we need a great deal of help."

There was a note of repressed desperation in this last speech, and as her relatives had really nothing better to do, Lillian agreed. But it was really quite an imposition. After the gentlemen had left, Lillian explained what task had been foisted on them. Martha could not have found a job more to her liking—to have an excuse to go into every shop and complain of its wares. To be consigning turnips to the poorhouse and potatoes to the orphans and deciding who should get six ells of cotton—only see how poorly it was bleached, good for nothing but dustrags— and all without having to spend a penny, was her idea of heaven.

"Mr. Fellows is certainly a remarkably generous man," she repeated several times as she went from shop to shop, identifying herself as "here on behalf of Mr. Fellows of St. Christopher's Abbey, the Whig candidate." She could not say as much for his wisdom in paying so much money for such shoddy goods, and added an aside to Sara,

"You'll have to keep a sharp eye on the purse strings when you are married. He has no management, no economy, but he is remarkably generous."

At the end of the long afternoon, Sara turned to Lillian with a soft smile. "Look what Mr. Alistair gave me," she said, and offered her cousin a pamphlet. It was a Tory bulletin, puffing their candidate and mentioning the party's platform. "He gave me a whole pile of them for my friends, and I have been leaving one in each shop we were in."

"Oh Sara, he's a Tory!"

"Papa was a Tory. That's why he asked me if I would like to do it."

"But we are working for Mr. Fellows!"

"That's nice. *I* am working for Mr. Alistair," Sara said, and gazed meaningfully at the pamphlet with all the terribly hard words in it that she couldn't make heads or tails of.

She handed Lillian her next-to-last one and her cousin accepted it with some eagerness to see what she could learn of Mr. Alistair. She chucked it quickly into her purse to be read at home, for if Aunt Martha ever discovered what Sara had been up to, she'd skin her alive.

# 5

WHETHER through courtesy or for a lack of friendly homes in which to parade his candidate, Mr. Hudson stopped with Fellows at New Moon again the next morning on his way into the village. He thanked the ladies for distributing the charity goods and again for addressing the envelopes. He appeared a little depressed, but Fellows was in high gig, bragging to Sara about the fine showing he had made the night before at the Veterans' Hall when he met the grain-growers.

"We had a marvelous turnout," Fellows said. "Every grower for ten miles around was there to hear me speak. But I didn't toady up to them as Alistair did. I stood my ground like a good Whig and laid into them for their greed, wanting to keep all the money for themselves. Money is the root of all evil, and I begin to think grain is the next worst root."

"Do you not grow grain yourself?" Martha asked.

"Certainly I do, but I don't insist on ten shillings a bushel for it. Mind you, it is the going rate this year as a result of the Corn Laws. It is the Corn Laws that have given us such a good price, and it wouldn't do to undersell my neighbors, but I hope I am not greedy. I have seen the light and am no longer a Tory. And when I am elected I mean to repeal the Corn Laws. An ounce of prevention is worth a pound of cure."

"What do you mean?" Martha asked.

"Why—why—repealing the Corn Laws would prevent those repressive Tories from selling at ten shillings a bushel!"

"I trust that was not the tenor of his speech to the grain-growers!" Lillian said to Mr. Hudson in a low voice. He had the air of a man who wants to put his head in his hands and weep.

"You were right to warn me yesterday," he said.

"Did he make a very bad showing?"

"He made wretched work of it. Just what you are hearing now, and worse. It had to be to the farmers he delivered what he was dipping into at Allingham's yesterday. We'll have to keep party literature from him."

"But you mean to run a good clean campaign, Mr. Hudson. He could hardly claim to be in favor of the Corn Laws."

"He could have explained why we are against them. The poor must be fed, and if their wages don't enable them to buy food with the high cost of it due to this law, then the money must come from the parish dole, and where does that money come from but the wealthy of the parish? They give with one hand and take with the other. Better to sell their grain at a fair market price than to hike it up with duties on imported grain and put food beyond the reach of the working man. Every man is entitled to earn a fair wage. No one wants to be a beggar, and it must go against the pluck for a man who works sixteen hours a day to have to stand in line and beg for his bread."

"Mr. Fellows said nothing of that?" she asked, well-impressed with his words and principles, and particularly with his impassioned manner of delivering them.

"He knows nothing of it, and he's a grain-grower himself. But I don't mean to disparage him; his intentions are certainly good. He is an honest man. Perhaps he is too honest for this game."

"Maybe you should give him a hand with his speech-writing till he gets on to it," she said, feeling this idea might not sit well with Mr. Hudson.

"I wrote him a good speech. That is, we worked it out together, you know. But Alistair threw himself open to questions from the floor and Fellows followed his lead. It was during the unrehearsed question period that he went all to pieces. Reising put Alistair up to it, I fancy. He sized Tony up pretty well yesterday. Last night was a total disaster for us, but we hadn't much hope for the farm vote in any case. I hope our jaunt to the village yesterday did some good with the merchants."

Lillian hadn't the heart to tell him what Sara had been up to. "I'm sure it did. All the things you bought and gave to the poor must have given the tradesmen a good opinion of your candidate."

"That's pretty well standard procedure. Reising would have done the same. One can't afford *not* to do it."

He then turned to hear what Fellows was saying to the other ladies. ". . . and if they don't watch out we'll have a whole nation of beggars," he finished up, still discussing his speech. "Isn't that right, Matthew?"

"The grain-growers certainly won't be beggars, as Alistair pointed out. I think it is the matter of all taxes ultimately coming out of the pockets of those who make more than a living wage you should stress. They are robbing Peter to pay Paul, the way they go about it."

"Ho, the Tories would rob anyone," Tony replied. "And Peter Peckham is the worst of the lot. But as to paying Paul, he'll keep the whole lot for himself."

"Who is Peter Peckham?" Hudson inquired, dazed.

"Why, robbing Peter as you just said. He would rob from his own mother if he were given half a chance."

"No, no, that was not my meaning."

"Oh, well, I know you don't want any *ad hominem's,* but as you mentioned Peter Peckham yourself, and we are among friends, there is no harm in saying the fellow is a scoundrel. I wouldn't trust him with a brass farthing. He is a sly one. But then it takes one to know one, as they say."

"Oh ho, so you are a sly one too, eh, Mr. Fellows?" Martha joked him. He looked grossly offended at this effort to read meaning into his words.

A confused discussion followed, during which Mr. Hudson tried once again to inculcate into Mr. Fellows's mind his reasons for being against the Corn Laws, and at the termination of his labor Sara said, "I think you are all wrong."

She had an attentive audience, for she rarely spoke out in such a firm voice and never on a serious matter. "The Tories only want to stop other countries from dumping their grain on us." She had been much struck with the phrase in the pamphlet, wondering where those countries would dump it, and thinking how odd it would look— great stacks of grain sitting about the countryside.

"Bless me, where did you learn such a thing, love?" her mother asked, very proud of her. "Your papa was used to say that very thing. Only think, she remembers that from her father, and Gerald in his grave over a year."

This was Mr. Hudson's first indication that the Tory element in the house was still active, and he looked a question at Martha.

"Gerald always talked a deal of nonsense. Have no fear, gentlemen. We are on your side."

"That is an old Tory idea—that countries are dumping their excess grain on us—but when our own harvest was poor, as it was last year and this, it should not be called dumping, but honest trading. God knows we export enough products to other countries." He addressed these remarks to Tony, but his candidate was looking elsewhere, for he was once again struck by Sara's beauty.

"It's unusual to find brains and beauty in a lady," he congratulated her.

"Oh, I am not at all clever, Mr. Fellows," she objected.

"What you just said about dumping—that was clever."

"No, Tony, that was *not* clever, as I have just been explaining," Hudson told him. "It is very shortsighted."

"I meant clever for a lady," Tony said, with a condescending look at the four women. "But a woman's place is in the home, what? Shall we be off to spend more of the old *sine qua non's?*" he asked. Hudson rubbed his brow in a weary fashion and said that they had better spend a great deal, and they were off.

Miss Monteith had come to New Moon to get Sara married, and as the groom was to be in the village spending his patrimony, she shepherded her charges in that direction after lunch. Lady Monteith stayed home, as it was not her custom to budge an inch unless it should be necessary.

The groom was not seen, since Hudson had taken him to visit Basingstoke and the families who lived to the West, but Martha discovered two items of interest, one of which inflamed her to wrath. There was to be a large political rally three evenings hence, and its significance to her was that Mr. Fellows would not be able to dine with them on that evening. The other news was that Mr. Alistair was a criminal even if he hadn't a record, and so she would warn Mr. Fellows accordingly. His crime was that he was corrupting the merchants of Crockett.

She overheard Mr. McGillicutty, the cobbler, say with a laugh that he had never got twenty-five pounds for a pair of boots before, and she stood examining a pair of leather laces till this interesting piece of information should be explained to her satisfaction. She imagined him to be fashioning some marvelous footgear for the royal family, but no. It was soon revealed that Mr. Alistair was paying the cobbler twenty-five pounds for a plain pair of boots without even a white band to the top of them, and if *that*

was not corruption she was a wet goose! Her fiery eyes
let it be known to her nieces how far from a wet goose
she considered herself to be.

"But Mr. Fellows paid a crown for a bushel of turnips,
Aunt Martha, and no one ever paid more than a half-
crown before," Sara pointed out.

"Charity—that is a different matter. Certainly he was
taken in on the price of turnips—I mentioned it myself—
but it was an error, not bribery. Twenty-five pounds for
a pair of topboots is a very different matter. Mr. Fellows
will hear of this, and Mr. Alistair will stand revealed for
the low, criminal conniver he is. I didn't like the looks of
him from the beginning. *He grins.* Never trust a man that
grins, girls. Let it be a lesson to both of you."

"I like the way he grins," Sara said softly.

"He'll grin on the other side of his face when Mr.
Fellows gets after him," Martha replied.

Miss Watters rather thought it would be Mr. Hudson
who would get after him; she had no doubt that the
gentleman of high morals would put a speedy end to
bribery and corruption in the village.

Martha went home immediately and sent a footboy off
to St. Christopher's Abbey requesting Mr. Fellow's's im-
mediate—underlined twice—attendance on her regarding
a most important matter. It suited her well to have such
a good excuse to lure him back to New Moon, where she
had every intention that he should remain for dinner and
the evening. Nor did she have the least objection if Mr.
Hudson should accompany him, for he had been seen to
drive about the countryside in a very dignified black carriage drawn by a matched team of bays. She had observed
as well that he had more than one well-cut coat to his
back, and a fine gold watch. (There appeared to be some

sort of a crest on the watch, but her hopes had not soared to the height of thinking he had any right to the crest. There was still enough lowness in him that he might have won it in a card game.)

"You, Lillian, can help me keep Mr. Hudson occupied so that Sara may have a minute alone with Mr. Fellows. A little privacy in a far corner is all I mean, of course, for certainly we shan't leave the room. Even the best of men, as Mr. Fellows certainly is, is not to be entirely trusted."

"I look forward to speaking to Mr. Hudson again. He is the more sensible of the two, I feel."

"He's sharp as a tack, I have no doubt, but don't get to dangling after him, my dear, for we really don't know a thing about him. He cannot be a man of much means or he wouldn't be doing this low sort of clerical work for Mr. Fellows, but would have a place of his own to look after. I wonder if the party supplies him with a team for his work." This possibility, just occurred to her, sent Mr. Hudson down a notch. "A bird in the hand is worth two in the bush, and Mr. Thorstein is interested in you."

"You are learning a trick from Mr. Fellows, I see, throwing platitudes at me, but you must not give them quite so much point." Lillian made no mention of Mr. Thorstein's having twice offered for her and twice being rejected, but accepted quite happily her evening's job.

Martha's plan of getting the gentlemen to dinner did not work, however. They did not arrive till eight, and Mr. Hudson mentioned being very busy, giving a glance at his interesting crested watch as though he considered even this late visit an inconvenience.

Martha, who soon usurped the hostess's role in whatever home she visited, saw the gentlemen seated with a glass of wine in their hands before she exploded her bomb regarding the bribery Mr. Alistair had brought to Crockett.

"By Jove!" Mr. Fellows said, and glanced to Hudson for a clue as to how he should feel about this outrage.

"Up to that old trick, are they," Hudson commented, neither outraged nor even surprised, to judge from his sardonic smile. "It isn't the first time, believe me."

"I'm sure Mr. Alistair never corrupted anyone before," Sara told him with a very earnest face.

"Alistair? No, no, this is Reising's doing. Twenty-five pounds, did you say, ma'am?"

"Exactly, and they weren't worth a guinea or anything near it. Shoddy work."

"Mr. Alistair never wears shoddy boots!" Sara exclaimed.

"He has a shoddy way of buying them," her aunt said sharply. "What do you mean to do about it, Mr. Fellows?"

"I never buy my boots from McGillicutty. I buy in London," he informed her, with a smug smile at his cunning. "If Alistair wants to throw away his *sine qua non*'s on shoddy boots, well, *caveat emptor*, eh, Matt? If the shoe fits, wear it."

Sara frowned in confusion at such hard talk, and felt strongly inclined to defend Mr. Alistair further.

"What do you mean to do about your opponent sinking to bribery, I mean?" Martha asked, not yet quite angry but becoming definitely impatient.

"I wouldn't do a thing," Hudson said. Fellows immediately nodded his head in approval, but Miss Monteith and Lillian were amazed.

"You don't mean to let him get away with it!" Lillian said. "You wanted an honest campaign, Mr. Hudson. Oh,

I see what it is. You will not lower yourself to reveal publicly what he has done, but in private surely you will have a word with him—warn him you will not tolerate such finagling as this."

He observed her closely as she spoke with some unreadable expression on his face—a little surprise perhaps, a little smile, and possibly a bit of cunning. "I assure you, Miss Watters, I don't mean to let him get away with it. Have I not already had occasion to tell you I have my wits about me?"

Mr. Fellows was telling the other ladies in his resonant, speech-making voice that he never bought a stitch of his clothing or a stick of his furniture or anything else in this pokey little town, for there wasn't a decent craftsman in the whole area, and they all charged as much as you'd pay for decent goods in London.

Hudson heard him out, then decided that he must be set straight at once. "It will be your responsibility, after you are elected, Tony, to praise your village as the finest corner in England, inhabited by the cleverest craftsmen, with the best produce and weather and all the rest of it. Begin by buying locally—that is the least the merchants can expect of you, the man they mean to send to London. How are they going to know of Crockett and its problems in the city if their M.P. is not praising the town wherever he goes."

"They'd laugh me to scorn if I went off to London wearing Jed McGillicutty's coarse old boots, or Frank Saunders's misshapen hats. How am I to be entertaining ministers and lords in my home if I haven't a decent stick of furniture or good food on my table?"

"Publicly and locally, however, you must seem to be enchanted with your town or it will not be enchanted with you, and vote for you, and send you off to London as the Honorable Anthony Fellows, M.P., to represent it in Parliament."

The magic Honorable and M.P. did the trick. "Just buy their old junk and wear it around the village, you mean?" Mr. Fellows asked, wondering whether he could sink himself so low, for in spite of his talk of London, he rarely went near it; it was the locals' opinion of him that he considered important. Of greatest importance was that he be thought a cut above them all—a gent who had a London tailor. What a dilemma!

"I mean buy the excellent wares of Messrs. McGillicutty and Saunders and others, and be seen to wear them."

"Heh heh—look a dashed quiz," Tony said to Sara.

"Mr. Alistair bought McGillicutty's boots and he would never wear shoddy boots," Sara assured him, but was not curious enough or interested enough to once cast her eyes down to see what sort of boots Mr. Fellows had on.

All this was fine, but Martha was soon back demanding to know precisely what was to be done about the corruption. As she put her question to Fellows, Miss Watters listened with interest.

"Matthew will think of something," Tony assured them, causing them to look to Mr. Hudson for information.

"I have thought of something," Hudson told them, "and it's time we got busy and did it. We also have to go over the items that are likely to arise at the public meeting. Shall we go, Tony?"

Tony rose obligingly to make his adieux.

"Twenty-five pounds, you said, Miss Monteith?" Hudson queried Martha as they left.

"Twenty-five pounds. I was shocked," she told him.

"I am a little surprised at the sum myself," he said with a smile.

"I do believe Alistair is beginning to see the light," Tony put in. Only Sara followed his rambling reasoning.

"He must have become a Whig!" she said at once. "He is no longer keeping all the money for himself."

It was noticed by Martha and Lillian that Mr. Hudson's lips were unsteady when Tony said to him, "Told you she was a deuced clever girl," but till he was out the door he did not allow himself to lose control.

After they had left, Lady Monteith poured herself a glass of ratafia and said, "That's taken care of. Mr. Fellows will do something."

"You're a goose, Melanie. It is Mr. Hudson who will do something," Martha informed her. "Fellows may be the candidate, but it becomes clear it is Mr. Hudson who is running the show."

Lillian thought it had been clear for some time. She listened with amusement while Martha continued, "At least Mr. Hudson is a proper sort of a gentleman. Not well off, but I daresay he may be from a good family for all that—a younger son, you know. He means to take steps to see the corruption is stopped. I wonder what he will do."

The Rubicon was passed. Authority was in Mr. Hudson's hands; he was somebody. She didn't yet know precisely who, but his carriage was allowed to be his own from that moment on, and the watch, likely a gift from his family who possessed a crest and the right to have it emblazoned on a watch for a younger son if they chose.

Never one to shilly-shally, Martha had set a date for the tea party, and the next morning she had the three females gathered around her to make up a list and address cards. It proved a more difficult chore than she had imagined, for Sara and Melanie between them couldn't remember a dozen names offhand. They had to be taken for a mental drive down each street and lane to aid their memory. "Who lives in that fine old half-timbered place on the corner?" Martha asked Sara.

"The McLaughlins. They will want to come, to be sure. We must ask them or they will be vexed." Then, as the envelope was being addressed, she added, "Only of course she is Mr. Alistair's sister, and might not want to come to a Whig party." She felt dashing indeed to be giving a political party, with such deep and cunning matters as this to consider.

"Peagoose!" Martha declared bluntly, crumpling the envelope. "What about your churchman here? What is his name and should we ask him?"

"We must certainly ask Dr. Everett. He would be shocked if we did not. He loves a tea party."

"Is *he* any kin of the Alistairs?" Martha asked ironically.

"No indeed, he does not care for Mr. Alistair in the least since he wouldn't give a penny for the fuel fund to cover the cost of the coal last year. And his mama would not even go out and canvass."

"Mr. Hudson will want to hear of this!" Mr. Everett's card was set aside to be delivered in person. A minister of the church might be a powerful ally, if he were popular.

In this fashion the morning passed away, and by lunch they had a respectable stack of envelopes addressed. Sara was talked out of addressing a card to Mr. Alistair, and it seemed a great shame to her that a tea given at her house should be for the opposition when she herself had suddenly become a Tory. Seventeen years of Papa's talk had had no effect, but after Mr. Alistair had smiled at her she had become a secret Tory, with her pamphlet kept under her pillow, quite as dogeared as *Peter Pepper's Perfect Day*, though less thoroughly understood.

In the afternoon several of the cards were delivered in person by the ladies, who did a little discreet campaigning of their own consisting mainly of compliments for Mr. Fellows's appearance, manners, morals, and abbey, along with the rider that Mr. Hudson seemed a very nice gentleman too.

By 4:30 the ladies were home from delivering cards and had pretty well given up hope of any more excitement for the day when Mr. Fellows and his friend were announced. They came in carrying new hats in their hands.

"Mr. Hudson, have you taken care of that Tory corrupter?" Martha demanded.

"I think we've spiked his guns, and thank you for the tip, ma'am. How do you like our new *chapeaux*, ladies? Dashing, don't you think?" He put his hat on, as did Fellows. They looked not only inferior hats, but ill-fitting as well—Hudson's a little on the small side, so that it sat on the side of his head at a cocky angle, and Fellows's nestling more closely about the ears than a hat should.

"They're very nice," Sara said dutifully.

"I don't like it so well as your other, Mr. Hudson. I think I like your own hat better," Martha said, regarding the new hat judiciously. She reached out a hand for it and turned it upside down to examine the workmanship. "Why, the band is loose, and it has only a half-inch grosgrain around the brim. Not satisfactory at all! I hope you didn't pay much for it."

"I haven't paid anything yet. The price must depend on the outcome of the election."

Lillian narrowed her eyes suspiciously. When she glanced at Mr. Hudson, she saw he was smiling at her. "What is to be the price if Mr. Fellows gets in?" she asked.

"Fifty pounds."

"Fifty pounds!" Martha gasped. "Mr. Hudson, you must be mad."

"Oh no. If it, and Mr. Fellows's hat, prove such winning *chapeaux* that we are successful, I consider it a fair price."

"But that is bribery too!" Lillian charged.

"No, no, it is business. If the hat proves ineffectual, the cost is only a crown. Now that, you must own, is a perfectly appropriate price for a hat."

"And if you are willing to pay your crown for a hat, I suppose your soul is the price of Mr. Saunders's boots during an election campaign," Lillian said, sadly shocked that the august Mr. Hudson was not only a tyrant (she didn't really mind that too much) but a corrupter as well.

"No, the price for all raiments is the same—a hundred pounds for a pair of all we bought—boots, jackets, shirts. Fortunately we shan't be required to wear anything but the hats. They hadn't boots or jackets in stock to fit us."

"They didn't have hats either!" Lillian pointed out.

"No, but I feel Tony really ought to have at least a token of local produce about him, and the hats were not so uncomfortable as boots that pinched, or a jacket that pulled across the shoulders. It is the thought that counts."

"This sounds highly irregular, Mr. Hudson," Martha said, feeling almost faint as she realized what she was being told in the most brass-faced manner in the world. "It seems you are but another corrupter. You politicians are all alike."

"It is the regular custom, I assure you, ma'am, to grease the wheels a little during a campaign."

"But you were shocked that Mr. Alistair did it!" Sara objected.

"I was surprised that Reising was doling out only twenty-five pounds. I hadn't realized he was on such a tight budget. The word I had was that Sir John Sinclair had come down pretty heavily, to insure getting Alistair in. He looks to make a good profit from the bridge, if it is ever built, and the improvements on the roads too, as he owns the construction company that would get the contracts."

Martha had always known that the world of men was an evil place. Mr. Thorstein had spoken more than once to her in an oblique and incomprehensible manner of such things, but now she felt herself to be at the very center of them. This, then, was how they managed affairs. It was deplorable, of course, but it was the way of menfolk, and like their gambling and debauchery it was a thing a lady must turn a blind eye to and accept. It rather thrilled her after all to know her party was just as sharp as the other.

The amount of the bribes and the unconcerned manner of the disclosure led her to believe that Mr. Hudson dealt in higher figures than she had thought. (Corruption and bribery on such a scale she could not *help* admiring.) "How much has it cost you in round figures, Mr. Hudson?" she inquired in a worldly tone.

"Three hundred each," he said blandly.

"I see the election is a very good thing for the merchants," Lillian said. "They win, whoever gets in."

"Yes, they would be happy to see an election every year, no doubt, but the hats, I trust, will last us till the next general election."

"I'm sure they will. I doubt they will see much wear once the campaign is over," Lillian replied, eying Mr. Hudson's hat askance.

"But they will—all the things will serve as bribes to some unfashionable gents at the next by-election," Hudson told her, a glint of mischief in his eyes.

"You are just as bad as Reising and the Tories!"

"We call it good in politics, and either way we mean effective. There is no point trying to keep your hands entirely clean when you're in this business. This is going to be a very difficult election, and the Whigs sent their wiliest schemer—me."

"You sound proud of it."

"I'm not ashamed of it. The end justifies the means."

"A theory of Signor Machiavelli, if I'm not mistaken."

"Among other effectual gentlemen, yes. You call yourself a Whig—why do you dislike what I am doing? You know the Tories' record on the Luddite riots. If *Paris vaut bien une messe,* as one of the old kings said when he turned Catholic to gain France, then Crockett *vaut bien un chapeau un peu cher.*"

"*Très cher, et des bottes aussi.* But in French or English, it is bribery. You are corrupting innocent people."

This foray into French completely bewildered Fellows and Sara, who began to examine his hat with keen interest and to discover loose threads. "A stitch in time saves nine, what?" he remarked cleverly.

Hudson rose and went to join Lillian. Martha observed him as he seated himself at her side and turned to Melanie, her mind seething with conjecture and none of it political.

"Have I shocked you, Miss Watters? We are only continuing a long-established practice, and the merchants would be sore as boils if we didn't corrupt 'em a little.

Little thanks they'd give you for standing up for their virtue in this idealistic fashion. Ask them."

"Where are you getting all this money?"

"Various places."

"Tell me one. The man who pays the piper calls the tune, if I may borrow a cliché from your pupil."

"He'll never miss it. He has a hundred of them. And he is providing some of the blunt himself, so you see how wrong you are about calling tunes. Myself for another—and you know by now what a shy, retiring fellow *I* am in the matter of calling tunes. But of course the majority of it comes from the party coffers. The Whig aristocracy is wealthy—they can well afford to buy me and Tony a hat and a pair of boots."

"Yes, and no doubt they will be well-reimbursed for it by some sort of underhandedness if your party ever gets in."

"You have all the makings of a fine politician, ma'am. I'm tempted to stick a beard and a pair of trousers on you and run you in the next by-election."

Lillian was a little surprised at the blunt, bordering on the crude, speech. She had thought from his rather stiff appearance he would be more formal, especially with a lady.

"I could use the new wardrobe. I daresay I'd have a closetful of gowns before it was over."

"No, no—trousers! But I have the notion that's what you'll be wearing after you're married—or trying to," he said, quizzing her.

"You find me a managing female?"

"I find you delightful as always, Miss Watters. A regular ray of sunshine."

To hear the high-principled Mr. Hudson flash from

informality to outright flirtation after his descent into corruption was too much for Miss Watters to assimilate. She sat stunned, while he ran on nonchalantly. "And as usual, I can take only a brief exposure to your salutary rays, but I feel the goodness of them all day long. A man in the corrupt line of business that I am in needs to be reminded there are still innocent souls in the world." He smiled warmly, casting a golden glow of his own.

"I expect it is nearly your dinner time," he said. "We only came to show off our new hats. Did I shock your aunt, do you think? I know I shocked you. I ought not, perhaps, to have said anything, but if you are to continue helping us, it is better to drop you the hint we are not so immaculate as she thought us—you all thought us."

"I was surprised my aunt's objections were not more strenuous. But she is violently anti-Tory and must consider no trick too low if it will beat them."

"And you? Do *you* feel it was an awful thing to do? It is done all the time, by all parties."

"Two wrongs don't make a right, or a dozen or a hundred wrongs either."

"No, but they might get the right candidate elected. Will you continue to support us?"

She wondered whether it was a request or only a question. "I suppose, as Mr. Reising started it, you hadn't much choice."

"If *he* hadn't started it, I would have. He is spending very lightly—he must think he's got this seat sewed up. Twenty-five pounds is an insult."

"Perhaps he paid another twenty-five for the polish for the boots?"

He smiled rather lazily. "I have to try to pour a whole lifetime's education into Mr. Fellows in the few days before that meeting. We really must go. I look forward to seeing you again soon." There was something in his voice or expression that made her feel she was being singled out for special attention. As he turned to Fellows and Sara, Lillian's eyes followed him.

"Really a pretty fine hat," Mr. Fellows was saying, holding it up and regarding it with admiration. "I daresay it might be taken for a Baxter, but I'll be sure to tell them at Whitehall it was made by Saunders of Crockett."

Hudson glanced at Lillian, who could scarcely control her laughter. "I didn't expect him to bother quoting me in this house, where my first lecture was overheard," he said.

"You put him up to that!"

"Only to please Saunders. He is more likely to send Fellows to London if he thinks he will be a walking advertisement, you know."

"I know this campaign is not going to be as lily-pure as you let on. Already we have been subjected to bribery and outright lies."

"And I've only been here three days! What might I not be up to in the next three weeks?"

"If I hear of a number of corpses littering the streets of Crockett, I shall know where to look for the murderer."

"Only if they're Tory corpses. Come along, Tony, back to work. No rest for the wicked."

"He's only funning, you know," Tony assured the ladies. "It's the Tories who are wicked, but we'll show them. And when I go up to London to represent Crockett I will say that Crockett has the prettiest girls in England too, as well as the best craftsmen, right, Hudson?"

"Right, Tony." He smiled to see that Sara did not object to having her staggering beauty debased to the level of perfection of Mr. Saunders's hat. But the other sharp-eyed little filly was laughing behind her prim lips. He winked at her and watched in amusement as she let on not to see it, glancing away quickly and then back at him with a questioning frown.

# 6

AUNT Martha's pursuit of Mr. Fellows as a husband for Sara was by no means abated upon her discovering that he was a fool. In fact, his mentality was exactly suited to Sara's own. She couldn't think of anyone else who could tolerate either of them. She could seldom dislodge Lady Monteith from the house in the pursuit, but the girls were always happy to go into town, and Crockett was becoming a very interesting place these days. With all the merchants having so much extra money in their pockets, spirits were lively all over, and any day it was four pence to a groat that one or the other or even both of the candidates would be seen there in the midst of a group, laughing, talking, and shaking hands—usually at some point in the day strolling into the Cat's Paw for a meal or to stand a round of drinks.

Both candidates and their whippers-in considered themselves on fine terms with the ladies from New Moon, and would stop to chat with them if it was possible, but two days passed without Hudson and Fellows again calling at the house. In the interim, a Tory meeting took place at the Veterans' Hall, and one of the pieces of news heard in the town later was that the meeting had become rather rough. Mr. Alistair had been pelted with rotten apples, presumably not by Tories. But of course no one had so low opinion of either Tony or Hudson as to feel they were involved in it. It was some local people of the lower classes, and it was disgraceful.

Between visits to Crockett and the surrounding countryside, Hudson and Fellows worked together in an effort to make Fellows conversant with the principles of his party. Having had a Tory father all his life, he had an unfortunate tendency to spout off Tory ideas. Mr. Hudson was worried about the large public meeting to be held at the Town Hall. On the day of the meeting, they stopped at New Moon and were of course asked how the campaign was going.

"We've got them on the run," Fellows said happily. "You heard about the rout at the Tory meeting? Alistair was *rompéed* entirely. He'll not get a vote come November first, depend on it. If he was boo'd at a Tory meeting of corn-growers, you may imagine what his chances are tonight, when *my* supporters are out in force."

"Mr. Alistair said it was the Whigs who threw the apples, Mr. Fellows," Sara told him. "I think if your supporters are to be there tonight, you had better both be careful, for it was the Whigs who threw the rotten apples."

"Nonsense!" he said indignantly. "It was a *Tory* meeting. What would *my* men have been doing there?"

"The Whigs threw apples at Mr. Alistair, and it was not very nice," she insisted, pouting.

"But why should his own men pelt him with apples?" Lillian asked, with a suspicious eye in Mr. Hudson's direction. There was a sparkle in his gray eyes as he lifted a brow at her that she did not quite trust.

"Why, the Tories are so stupid they don't know the difference," was Tony's explanation of the affair.

"It looks as if it might be a rough meeting tonight," Lillian said, turning to Mr. Hudson, who had seated himself beside her upon entering, a mark of distinction both noticed and felt by her.

"I look forward to a lively débacle," he said with a conspiratorial smile, and then, speaking in a low voice, presumably to spare Tony, "Rotten eggs, cat-calls—the whole cat, in fact, flung in his face."

"There were dead cats thrown in the West Riding. Disgusting! Will it be likely to happen here?"

"I consider it almost inevitable. Keep a sharp eye on your domestic brindle or she'll end up on Alistair's—or Fellows's—shoulders."

"Mr. Fellows won't stick it, Mr. Hudson. He stands too high on his dignity for such rough treatment."

"He looks forward to the honor. I have prepared him."

"No, not even you could accomplish that."

"You have a low opinion of my powers of persuasion, ma'am. Listen to him; he's giving your aunt my lecture now. Please allow for its mangling at his hands."

They both looked toward Mr. Fellows, who was holding forth in his resonant voice. "It will be rough going tonight, but politics is for men, not boys. You can always expect to come in for abuse when you stand up for something. The bishop of London, Lord Castlereagh and all the outstanding men of the times were abused and vilified during the Corn Riots. Their windows were broken and mud and stones were flung at them in the streets. Even the Prince of Wales knows well enough how it is—he dare not go in the streets for fear of being pelted with garbage. I will be in good company. But I will take it all with dignity."

Lillian turned to Hudson with a sapient eye. "What is the *dignified* way to take a dead cat being thrown at you?" she asked.

"It involves a deal of ducking and dodging."

"It sounds monstrously dignified. Your Mr. Fellows is not noticeably lightfooted. You may have talked him into accepting it mentally, but what will happen when he is faced with the reality of it? He'll cry craven and bolt on you, Mr. Hudson. Depend on it."

"I'll reinforce him with another bout of lectures before we go and circulate some fellows amongst the audience to lift any suspicious brown bags they see. I have half a dozen flash culls from the east side of London arrived today."

"What on earth are flash culls?" she demanded.

"Petty criminals," he answered, unmoved. "Excellent

for this sort of work, and it keeps them out of real mischief. Mind you, there's one in the bunch is on the ken lay—ah—a housebreaker, in genteel parlance. Have an eye to your silver and jewelry for the next few days."

"You employ common criminals in your work?" she gasped.

"Shh!" he said with a nervous glance at the rest of the group. "Let them recover from my corruption before they hear of this. They are not really bad fellows at all, I assure you. I find them totally reliable. There was a list of names I absolutely had to get hold of at the last general election, and my own best efforts at burgling the gent's room came to nought, so in desperation I hired a gallows-bird . . . oh dear, I've lost you again. I hired a pickpocket to filch it from the man's pocket for me. He put me in touch with a few other flash culls and I find their skills very useful."

"Upon my word, you are shameless!" she said, but in a low voice, to help him conceal his conduct.

"You wrong me. I am very much ashamed of myself," he answered her with mock humility.

"You said it would be a clean campaign!"

"And so it will be. Throwing dead cats, you must admit, is not a gentlemanly thing to do."

"I suppose you had nothing to do with the rotten apples that littered the stage of the Veterans' Hall after last night."

"I heard something about that . . ."

"Yes, before it happened, I haven't a doubt."

"I did happen to hear Farmer Squibb had a barrel of windfalls that were going bad on him. I hate to see good food wasted, don't you?"

"Especially at election time! There is another hundred pounds from the Whig coffers down the drain."

"No, on the platform at the Veterans' Hall. And he let me have them for twenty-five pounds. But we couldn't—didn't—catch any cats."

She stared at him openmouthed.

He laughed aloud. "I only said it to shock you. I never have dead cats thrown, for my mama was used to be fond of them. Rats occasionally, but . . ."

"Oh, that's worse than cats!"

"Killing them is not worse. Everyone hates rats, and it is usually considered a benevolent act to dispose of them. Don't tell me you like them?"

"Of course I don't like them! Nobody does, but that's no reason . . . Oh, you should be in chains and fetters, Mr. Hudson."

"I have an excellent picklock in my retinue, if that contingency should arise."

"As you never at *point non plus?*"

"I must confess I very nearly was yesterday. You'll never guess what little trick Tony played on me."

"What?" she asked, smiling in anticipation.

"Do you happen to recall our mentioning the other day a certain Sir John Sinclair, who is bankrolling the Tory campaign almost singlehanded?"

"Yes, the one who is going to build the bridge."

"Oh no, he isn't! But that is the one I mean all right. I was driving in all my naive innocence to strut Tony before a few scattered houses in the countryside, and he tells me he has a good friend at Ashley Hall—a fine old place, and the dame apparently on terms with him, so we stopped off to make ourselves agreeable, and who should live there but Sir John Sinclair! I thought he'd pull a gun from the wall and shoot us off the premises. He was livid, and who shall blame him! Can you see Alistair and Reising blundering into Allingham's place? But I blame myself entirely. I ought to have questioned him more closely as to the identity of the mysterious Lady Marie. Her being an earl's daughter and not using the title Lady Sinclair led me astray. She was once a flirt of Tony's, if I have the story straight. And what a woman she is—fat and ugly. I *was* at *point non plus*. You would have enjoyed to see me."

"What on earth did you say?"

"I asked for directions to the next farm, Wetterings. I let on we had lost our way, but old Sinclair didn't know what to make of it and thought we were up to something devious. With Tony simpering at Lady Marie and generally making an ass of himself, I believe he thought we went there bent on flirtation. I heard him lighting into her before we were out the door. Lord, what a day! Well, you learn something new in each campaign."

"What have you learned in this one?" she asked, laughing in glee at his having been discomposed for once.

"That lovemaking and campaigning are a poor mix."

"You'll have to shorten Fellows's rein."

"Yes, I'll have to keep an eye on him, too."

She looked startled at his last words, but refused to dwell on them. "So you received your comeuppance for once. I am glad to hear it."

"Yes, but if I succeed in getting Tony a set of letters after his name I'll be so set up in my own conceit there will be no bearing me."

"You are just about intolerable now."

"I know it well, and I want to tell you I appreciate your forbearance. I am not always so shamefully employed as you find me at the present moment. I am also a some-time estate manager, and I take very good care of my tenants and other dependents."

Lillian listened to this with interest, and was eager to hear what new attributes Mr. Hudson would acquire when her Aunt Martha was apprised of it. "I won't inquire how you go about it," she said.

"You would be amazed to hear how well they take to my overbearing ways. I haven't an enemy amongst the lot of them."

"They wouldn't last long if they were enemies. You'd whip them into line."

"I *am* the party whip, as well as Tony's whipper-in. His own particular brand of appellation, I might add. I don't think he quite understands the difference between my being a whip and a campaign manager on the side."

"You're a devil, is what you are. Utterly incorrigible."

"Possibly, but don't stop trying to correct me. I enjoy your lectures tremendously.

"I waste my breath, and I know it."

"Every golden syllable is heard."

"But not heeded."

"Remember the repressive Tories and the Luddite riots. And remember too to say a prayer for us tonight. We'll need it."

"I wish I could be at that meeting myself. A pity I hadn't that beard and trousers you spoke of the other day. But then election promises are writ on water."

"I wish I could take you. It will be too late to stop in afterward and describe it to you. We go on to the Cat's Paw to throw a shindig."

"More bribery—buying drinks for everyone."

"We'll stop by the next morning if you are really curious to hear how it goes."

"I am," she assured him. "I mean, we all are. Have you written Mr. Fellows's speech for him?" The pretense at collaboration was over.

"I'm in a dilemma. If I make him memorize a speech, he puts everyone to sleep with his dull way of rattling it off, with no pauses or emphasis or anything. He could put you to sleep reciting the most intriguing pornography. Well, I dozed off last night in the middle of *Les Crimes de l'Amour*, which he was reading to me . . ."

"Mr. Hudson! That is not a proper book for either of you to be reading."

"How do you know, Miss Watters, if you have not been dipping into the Marquis de Sade yourself?"

"I have not! But you said it was pornography!"

"It's *serious* pornography," he assured her, with a grave face and a mischievous eye. "But about my dilemma. Memorizing the speech is no good, and I have good reason to know that questions from the floor are fatal; Fellows turns Tory on me in mid-sentence. I've made up sheets of points to be made under various headings and I fervently hope that does the trick. Have you anything to suggest?"

She looked at Fellows, who was expatiating at length on the meal he had eaten at the Cat's Paw. "A wonderful saddle of mutton we had—tough as white leather, and the potatoes boiled to a pulp. I had heartburn all evening long."

"Only think if he had had a *good* meal!" Lillian said to Hudson.

"He hasn't quite got the knack of praise yet. He thinks

he may run things down as much as he likes, as long as he prefaces it with a compliment first."

"You have got yourself an admirable candidate—an excellent man. It's a pity he has neither wit nor principles."

His lips twitched. "I *will* buy you a mustache and a pair of trousers one of these days. Your brains are wasted in a lady's head. Come, put them to work. How am I to put him over this evening?"

"I don't think it is quite a proper or honest thing to suggest, but—is there someone you could trust to ask him specific questions for which you could prepare him? I mean, if he *knew* in advance what the questions were to be, maybe you could jot down points and let him use his own words. Maybe—maybe those flashing culls you mentioned, for I don't think you should let the local people know what you're up to."

"You're marvelous," he said.

She blinked in surprise and then feared she was blushing as well.

"You have saved the day, or night, for me, Madame Machiavelli. Was this done in the West Riding, or did this piece of deceit come from your own head?"

"I thought of it myself. It isn't really *dishonest*. It is just giving him the chance to put forth his views."

"Excellent rationalizing. You wouldn't care to help me chase rats this afternoon?"

"Have your flashing culls do it. It will keep them out of mischief. Worse mischief, I mean."

"That's *flash* culls, Miss Watters. If you're going to patter flash with me—speak thieves' cant—you had better get the idiom straight. Between teaching Tony Latin and you flash I'll be forgetting my own English."

"And then there are the Marquis de Sade's French stories to further confuse you."

"Oh no, we are reading that in English translation."

"Well, you shouldn't be!"

"I agree it is better to read the book in its original language when possible, but Tony's copy has been put into English . . ."

"You know that's not what I meant!"

"Too late. I took you for a Bath Miss when I first met you, with your implying I should not mention Alistair's *criminal record*, but I am coming to have a better idea of you now. I mean better in both its senses, in case you wonder—clearer and improved both. You are up to all the rigs, Miss Watters."

Lillian felt as highly complimented by this praise of her skill in deceit as if he had given her a real compliment. She realized, after the gentlemen had left, that her own moral principles stood to be in some jeopardy from this gentleman with the noble face of a judge and the mind of a common criminal.

"What had Mr. Hudson to say, Lillian?" Martha asked her.

"Just talking about the meeting tonight. He fears it may be rough."

"I expect it will. And by the by, Lillian, it isn't necessary for you to so monopolize Mr. Hudson when he calls. We would all like a word with him. When I hinted you might help to entertain him, I didn't mean for you to make it a full-time job. He *seems* well enough, but we really know very little about him."

"We were just talking about politics. He is well-informed; it is a pleasure to speak to a gentleman who knows exactly what is going on."

"I noticed you took no small degree of pleasure in his company. That won't do—won't do at all—at least not till we find out more about him. Try if you can find out where he's from."

"He mentioned an estate and tenants," Lillian said with satisfaction.

"Did he, indeed! How large? Where?"

"I must have some more private conversation with him to find that out, but he is not always a whipper-in."

"A party whip, Lillian, is not a man who gets the candidates elected, but a highly respected gentleman who assembles the members for a vote and even manages them."

"I know. He mentioned something of the sort."

"You may be sure he has no real influence in the party. He is only some junior clerk . . ." Martha stopped, for she suddenly realized she was talking nonsense. Mr. Hudson might not be a man of great means, but he at least dealt in large sums of somebody's money, and was certainly not a junior clerk. "I'll have a chat with him myself next time he comes," she said.

"They will be stopping by tomorrow," Lillian told her.

"Will they indeed? Mr. Fellows did not say so."

"I don't think Mr. Fellows has much to say about anything, except such words as Mr. Hudson sticks into his mouth."

"Bless me! You don't suppose it's Hudson we should be getting for Sara, do you? It would be well to have one in the family with a little brains. You can look after yourself and don't require a sharp husband, but when I consider the way Mr. Fellows wasted his money on those wilted vegetables, I wonder if he is the right husband for Sara."

Sara listened in smiling silence to this discussion, as did her mother. "I like Mr. Fellows better," Sara allowed in a low tone to her mama. "He isn't so hard to talk to."

"He is very conversable, certainly," Lady Monteith told her daughter. She didn't really think so herself, but Martha had said so, and Gerald's sister knew everything.

7

<hr />

As promised, Hudson brought Fellows to New Moon in the morning to report on the meeting at the Town Hall. Mr. Fellows was in his usual optimistic mood, but Mr. Hudson seemed a trifle out of sorts. He wore a plaster under his left eye, and even before the ladies inquired into the success of the meeting, this had to be asked about.

"I ran into a door in the dark," Mr. Hudson said.

Before long, Fellows was off on his speech laboriously learned for the meeting and still remembered all these hours later. "We got right into it. My manager"—he smiled warmly at Hudson—"is the cleverest fellow that ever was. He knew every question that was likely to come up. They couldn't trip me up on a thing. By Jove, I wish I'd had you to help me prepare for Oxford, Matt. I gave them what-for about the way they're treating our veterans —'the bravest and best amongst us, the flower of our manhood, men who spilled their blood for their country and left behind them on foreign shores very real parts of themselves—often a leg or an arm or a nose!'"

"That's an eye, Tony," Matt corrected.

"Or an eye, and—dash it! you've thrown me off. Where was I? Oh yes, or an eye, and 'now come home to be treated like second-class citizens.' That went down pretty well, I can tell you. There was Jenkins sitting right in the audience with his leg left in France, and Coulter lost a boy in the Peninsula."

"*He's* a corn-grower, isn't he?" Matt asked.

"Yes, by Jove. And Harmer's lad too was in Spain— not killed, but a bit of a knock-in-the-head since he came back. Well, he was never a sharp lad, but he's taken to ducking behind carriages and houses—thinks he's dodging bullets still. A complete moonling he's turned into. Left his brains behind on Spain's foreign shore."

"We should be pushing that point stronger," Matt said. "I hadn't realized there were so many veterans in the community, and at least two of them grain-growers' sons. That wouldn't go down badly with them."

"Was there much violence at the meeting?" Martha asked.

"Very little," Fellows told her. "A bit of a scuffle outside, but in the hall itself there was no cat-throwing. Alistair got a few potatoes tossed at him, but only at the body. They missed his face."

"You mean somebody threw potatoes at Mr. Alistair?" Sara asked.

"He was not hurt at all," Hudson assured her.

"Who would do such a thing? Mr. Hudson, *you* are in charge of making it a clean campaign, and I hope you will look into this."

"I expect Reising is looking into it. It is his job to protect Alistair."

"I think he should get out of politics. It is too dangerous," Sara said, indulging in a frown.

"That's right, Miss Monteith," Fellows agreed. "Politics is for men, not boys, right, Matthew?"

"Right, Tony."

"Mr. Alistair is a man!" Sara asseverated. "But a *gentleman*, not a politician."

"It's a rough game," Fellows remarked, raking his memory without success for an epigram to clinch the matter.

With her aunt's injunctions regarding monopolizing Mr. Hudson's time fresh in her ears, Lillian was careful not to look too much in his direction, but she was aware all the same that he was looking at her, and when Martha began going over her list for the tea party with Fellows, he rose from his chair and came to join her on the sofa.

"How did it really go?" she asked him.

"Be kind to me—don't ask. Just let me sit here and bleed quietly on your lap."

"Another dead loss?"

"Not a total fiasco. He remembered the answers, but didn't always put them to the right questions. There seemed to be some confusion when he got to Peter robbing Paul's pocket to buy corn, but at least he didn't finger Peter Peckham as the culprit. I sweated buckets, as you may imagine. And the less said about the local bridge, the better. He unwittingly gives that major point to Alistair every time. Those tight-fisted Tories only reward their own, you know, and he neglects to mention that reward has not been forthcoming these ten years the old bridge has been down. Then too, he's really pleased as punch to be getting his ten shillings a bushel for his grain, so *that* point doesn't go over so well as it might with the nongrowers. But all things considered, it wasn't as awful as I feared, and it is you I have to thank for the idea of feeding him prepared questions."

"And what really happened to your eye? Did one of Reising's flash culls take a swing at you?"

"No, I actually was hit by a flying door. A big bruiser of a fellow threw it at me in that scuffle outside. And it was my door, too; I was the one who pulled it off its hinges to protect myself. But it's only a scratch. I nearly managed to dodge it entirely."

"It gives you a disreputable look you can ill afford. When anyone is so steeped in foul deeds as you are, he ought to keep up every semblance of respectability. I suppose that is why you walk around so stiffly and drive that solemn black carriage."

"I never before met a woman with such a natural instinct for this shady game as you have, Miss Watters," he congratulated, and she was not displeased with this left-handed compliment.

There was suddenly a soft shriek of delight from Sara. "We would love it of all things!" she said.

"It sounds very nice. We will be happy to go," Martha added, less intensely.

"I'm telling them about the assembly that you're calling a harvest ball, Matt," Fellows said. "Really only an excuse for us to get at the Tories in a social setting and see if we can open their eyes. You must all not let on it's Matt's party, for he's got a bunch—Basingstoke and some gentlefolk—he's pretending are running it, but it's really for me."

"An assembly, not really a ball, at the Assembly Hall in ten days' time. I hope you will all come," Hudson explained.

"And he's soaking everybody a guinea a couple to raise the *sine qua non*'s for my campaign," Fellows warned them.

"We are inviting the ladies of New Moon as our guests," Hudson added, disliking to have the price of their hospitality discussed so openly. "And a dinner is included in the price, so it isn't quite such a soaking as you say."

"Yes, but you're making all the Whigs' wives supply the dinner, then turning around and making them pay for it."

"Your bribery is turned upside down on you, Mr. Hudson," Lillian ventured.

"Involvement, that's the thing. Get them interested, and what are ladies ever interested in but balls and gowns."

"In men," Lady Monteith told him, her first contribution to the conversation.

"Oh well, if it's men you want, the assembly is the place for it. Politics is for men, not boys," Tony assured her.

"Will the Tories be there too?" Sara asked eagerly.

"Yes, Mr. Alistair will be there," Lillian replied.

"Is there something going on between her and Alistair?" Hudson inquired quietly.

"She would like there to be, and it does seem hard that you two Whigs should run tame in her house when her papa was always a Tory."

"That fact, amongst others, makes this house a particularly attractive one for us. It looks as though we have converted one Tory citadel."

"So that's why you keep popping in here!"

"I did say that reason amongst others. That the two loveliest girls in the neighborhood also live here doesn't help keep us two bachelors away. I rather thought your Aunt Martha was shoving Sara at Fellows's head. Am I mistaken?"

On every visit he surprised her. Today he was making free with their first names as though he had know them forever.

"It would be a suitable match. I doubt that anything will come of it."

"A dangerous pair."

"Whig and Tory, you mean?"

"No, idiot and imbecile. Both of them Tories at heart—what indiscretions might they not utter if they were too much together! Sara clammering for a bridge to get to Chepstow to shop, and Tony telling the world only a Tory can supply it. We must keep an eye on them. Oh, there is a sort of gala festival in town tomorrow night—dancing in the streets, refreshments and so on, some entertainment from London—jugglers and the like, I'm afraid. You must have heard of it. Will your Aunt Martha take you, or is it considered too common a frolic for young ladies?"

"How common a frolic will it be? I take for granted it is all your doing."

"No, you're out. It is Reising's party, and the harvest ball, as we are calling it, is my revenge. As it is a Tory affair, I don't hesitate to tell you it will begin by being common and end up a drunken brawl. I hope that won't keep you away, however."

"It sounds lovely. We might go early for the common part of it, but Auntie will surely draw the line at a drunken brawl. We shall miss the best part," she said archly.

"If it is the lack of male escorts in the house to take you, I will be happy to offer Fellows and myself."

"You will be busy making up to Tories and other unenlightened persons, but we will see you there, I expect."

"You may be sure you will. A pity you couldn't stay for the dancing, but we have Tony's ball to look forward to."

Lillian knew she was devoting more time to Mr. Hudson than her aunt would approve of, so she turned her attention to the larger group. Still, she did not escape censure later when her Aunt Martha found she had been so negligent as to turn the private talk to no good purpose. She could not report where Mr. Hudson's estates were to be found, nor the extent of them, nor even if he was a younger or elder son.

But her condemnation was not absolute, for there were two parties to be prepared for and anticipated, and of course these would provide opportunities for closer questioning. With the daily trips to Crockett to watch the circus in progress there, time could not be said to drag.

It was always surprising to see Mr. Hudson and Fellows in converse with such lowly types in the village, talking to them with every sign of pleasure—not only the men, but women, too, who could by no stretch of the imagination be called ladies. Their both being bachelors was perhaps the reason for the women's interest. The number of lowly types increased markedly as the election drew nearer. The very day of the Tory frolic saw already a number of highly ornamented females whom Sara declared were not local residents, but local or not, they were on the best of terms with Fellows and his whipper-in.

Martha allowed her charges to attend the festival in the village and made Lady Monteith come along to help her chaperone, which resulted in her having to keep an eye on three rather than two, for Melanie was indiscriminate regarding the people she chose to mingle with. The main street had been closed off, with decorations and lanterns strung up to lend a holiday spirit. Everyone of both high and low degree turned out for the party, including a goodly number of dogs and cats and children who ought to have been in their beds. As free ale was on tap, there was no lack of insobriety even early on in the proceedings, and it seemed certain that before long there would be many staggering drunkards as well.

A band played on a platform set up in front of the Town Hall, where also a magician and three jugglers were performing various ingenious feats of legerdemain. Perhaps the more interesting sleight-of-hand tricks were going forward in the audience, where moneys and votes were exchanging hands as invisibly as the magician's rabbit vanished into his hat. Mr. Hudson was right there in the thick of it, surrounded by persons whom Lillian suspected of being flash culls—and not all male culls either. He appeared to take no notice of the party from New

Moon, but was in fact edging his way by degrees toward them, impeded by so many "friends" that his progress was slow. It took him half an hour to reach them, and Martha had about decided to take her three charges home. The show was over and a space being cleared for dancing.

"It was a mistake for us to come here," Martha said to the gentlemen. "It is a rowdy sort of a do. I'll take the girls home before they are accosted by ruffians."

"You won't want to stay much longer, but I see Lord Allingham working his way toward us. I would like to present him to you," Hudson said.

"Allingham, you say?" Fellows asked, looking about with an eager smile. "There he is, by Jove, coming right over to me."

He had soon reached them, and this oft-quoted gentleman was at last made known to them. He was a tall man somewhere in his sixties, with dignified white hair, a sweeping mustache, and wearing a monocle. He looked very out of place in evening clothes at this common country festival, though Fellows and Martha were happy to see him dressed as they believed a lord should be.

After he had been introduced, he expressed delight in making their acquaintance. It was Tony who performed the introduction, making Allingham known as "a *real* lord, an earl and the nephew of a duke, too, by Jove."

"And more importantly, a Whig, eh, Fellows?" Allingham added, laughing in embarrassment at such a gauche recital of his dignities. "How does it go, Matthew? Any chance at all of pulling the thing off?"

"I still have five hundred that says so," Matt told him. The two chatted between themselves, thus depriving Lillian of a much-anticipated tête-à-tête with Mr. Hudson.

Her only consolation was that he twice glanced at her and smiled while he talked to Allingham. He didn't say a private word to her, and she disliked very much what she managed to overhear him say to his lordship.

"You must make me known to Ratchett tonight. He is here, just back from London, I understand. An uncommitted vote."

"It ain't only his vote you're after, I bet."

"No, I want a little more than that from him. I hear he has a young daughter, quite pretty. I am anxious to meet her."

"That's Ratchett there, and got the young filly with him too. Handsome gel. We'll get on over there now."

They made their bows and left, while Lillian turned to Mr. Fellows to inquire who Mr. Ratchett might be.

"A Cit," was the condemning reply. "A rich merchant, full of grease—a low type. You wouldn't want to meet him."

A single glance at the gentleman, however, assured Miss Watters that he was one of the more civilized-looking persons present. His daughter was not only pretty but extremely modish. She curtsied to Mr. Hudson and was soon laughing and flirting with him. To hear her over the surrounding din, Hudson lowered his head toward her, looking at her with smiling admiration. She was a dark-haired, dark-eyed, vivacious girl. Lillian instantaneously felt a pang of jealousy that she told herself was fatigue, and suggested to her Aunt Martha that they leave at once.

"We haven't spoken to Mr. Alistair yet," objected Sara.

Mr. Fellows looked offended, and walked off toward Allingham and Ratchett, who were becoming a little parted from Hudson and the daughter.

"There is Mr. Alistair now," Sara suddenly said, and walked off to meet him, causing the three other women to follow in her wake, as they disliked to be without a male for protection. Mr. Alistair chatted with them for a few minutes and civilly offered to see them to their carriage before leaving.

"Is it true they threw potatoes at you, Mr. Alistair?" Sara asked as they walked along.

"Yes, Hudson had some troublemakers brought in, but Reising is up to anything. He let it be known there was free ale outside, and they all deserted the hall. There was a terrible fight outside—the constables finally managed to break it up. Hudson pulled a door right off its hinges when one of our boys went for him with a pitchfork. He is a great boxer, Reising says—floored Jackson in London. The handle of the pitchfork caught him a knock, but he didn't lose the eye."

This was not quite Hudson's version of the story, but close enough to it that Lillian had no doubt he was in the middle of the fight and very likely the ringleader.

"Were you hurt at all?" Sara continued.

"No, I am quicker on my feet that that. I caught a potato and threw it back. I see Hudson is making up to Ratchett's daughter. I'd give a monkey to know what he's up to. It's certain the heir to a barony is not planning to get himself buckled to a Cit's daughter. Did he say anything?"

"No, nothing," Sara told him.

Lillian, walking on Alistair's other arm, was sent reeling at this disclosure. "Mr. Hudson is heir to a barony, you say?" she asked.

"Yes—old Cecilford's heir. He is only a nephew, but

Cecilford has no sons, just two plug-ugly daughters. I fancy they plan to palm one of them off on Hudson if they can. He'll be inheriting any day; the old boy is eighty and the younger daughter nearly thirty. I wonder that Hudson bothers to embroil himself in a matter of this sort, for he has a dandy spread of his own in Kent. But they have been ardent Whigs forever, of course, and Brougham keeps him busy. He is putting up a tough fight, I can tell you. We thought this riding a shoo-in, especially with Fellows running, but Reising says Hudson is a devil and will stop at nothing. Well, here is your carriage, ladies." He smiled and was off.

"What do you make of that?" Lillian said to Sara, so overcome at Hudson's new eminence that she could hardly think straight.

"I didn't know you saw it," Sara answered shyly.

"Saw it? Heard it, you mean."

"No, no, he didn't say anything of interest, but he squeezed my fingers ever so tight before he left, and smiled."

No mention was made of either the squeezed fingers or the barony on the way home, and Lillian was not sure even then whether to tell her aunt. With a homely cousin and Miss Ratchett after Hudson, she had no desire for Martha to add Sara to the list. But Martha had heard intimations of Hudson's glory from other sources at the frolic, and brought it up at once.

"They are saying about town that Hudson is heir to Cecilford," she declared.

"Yes, Mr. Alistair told us so. What is a barony anyway?" Sara asked.

"It is a title, goose!" her aunt snapped, "and here we

have been wasting our time chasing that clothhead of a Fellows, when we ought to have been concentrating on Hudson. I'll tell you what to do, Lillian. Next time they come, you chat up to Fellows, and let Sara smile at Hudson."

"Maybe I would like to take a crack at a baron myself!" she answered hotly.

"You have been doing your best ever since we met him, but he paid no notice to you tonight. It was Miss Ratchett he was interested in. Thorstein is as well as caught—I had a note from him today inquiring after you. I often notice Hudson glancing toward Sara, smiling to himself. Anyone would be proud to have such a beautiful wife, even a fine, distinguished gentleman like Mr. Hudson. I suspected from the start he was no common clerk. You recall I mentioned early on that he was very clever . . . running the show, in fact. His tailoring, his carriage— everything about him of the first stare. He will want a wife, a beautiful wife, to set him off, and it is no matter that Sara is a ninnyhammer, for *he* has brains enough for two."

Mr. Hudson had finally been placed on the pinnacle where he belonged, and it seemed hard that now that he was acknowledged to be unexceptionable, she must hand him over to Sara. "Mr. Hudson might have something to say about that!" she said perversely.

"Do you think *you* can get him?" Martha asked with harrowing directness.

"No, Auntie, but perhaps Miss Ratchett can get him."

"Pooh—a Cit's daughter! That is only a flirtation to get Ratchett's vote or money for the campaign. He will look higher than that for a wife. He is using the chit. We have nothing to fear from her."

"He does *use* people," Lillian admitted sadly. Certainly he had used her—used her to address envelopes and direct the delivery of vegetables and to give him any ideas her poor brain could come up with. He had used her and used her badly, for he had not said a word to her the whole evening, but gone off in front of her eyes, flirting with Miss Ratchett.

"More power to him," was Martha's opinion. "And *we* shall use him to make a husband for Sara."

*8*

LILLIAN deduced the whipper-in had been to call at the rectory when Mr. Fellows took the stand for the reading in church the next morning. Whatever about his putting a body to sleep with reading pornography, he certainly managed to make the epistle soporific. Heads were nodding and eyes were glazed before he stepped down, but spirits revived after the service. The rector, well-pleased with the gift of a new desk and bookshelves for his study (especially as they were understood to be a private donation to himself, to go with him when he left— Hudson didn't miss a trick), was eager to show his pleasure. He had invited a party to the rectory for lunch, to be composed entirely of Whigs and uncommitted votes. But the crowd outside the church could not be let go without a little politicking, and both Alistair and Fellows were busy campaigning in a subdued, sabbatical way.

Lillian observed that while Fellows was caught up with some farmers, Hudson had edged his way toward the Ratchetts and was making himself pleasant to the family. Miss Ratchett was surely the most stylish lady in the congregation. She wore a fashionable green pelisse and a bonnet with black feathers. Lillian was possibly even happier than Sara when Mr. Alistair came up to speak with them, for she disliked to be seen standing about with no young man to lend her consequence.

In her pique she said, "I think *you* would have done the reading better, Mr. Alistair."

"I could hardly have done worse, could I?" he laughed, delighted with praise from the girl he privately considered Hudson's flirt.

"No, indeed you could not, and I think you should speak to Dr. Everett about taking the stand next Sunday."

"This is strange talk for a Whig supporter. Has Miss Sara been giving you our literature?"

"She did give me a copy of your pamphlet, and I read it with interest. I think you make some good points too."

"Lillian is very clever," Sara warned him.

He looked at Lillian with interest. "I hope her cleverness will remove the scales from her eyes and lead her to a more proper view in politics."

"Oh, but it is the Whigs who have seen the light!" Sara told him, with no notion that she might be causing offense.

"Now that is the sheerest folly!" Alistair laughed. They talked on and soon began to excite interest in those around them, for the handsome young Tory candidate was usually observed pretty closely wherever he went. Hudson looked twice in their direction, and was soon making a graceful bow to the Ratchetts and hastening his steps toward the group.

"Are you poaching on my territory, Mr. Alistair?" he asked with a smile that divested the question of ill humor.

"Oh, as to that, I consider charming young ladies free territory till they are officially claimed, Mr. Hudson. I am not *always* bent on politics, you know, as *you* seem to be. Don't be led into believing Mr. Hudson cares for anything but your politics, ladies."

"We are not so deceived in him, Mr. Alistair," Lillian assured the Tory. "We have enough chance to observe him that we know pretty well what he is up to."

"One would take me for a candidate to hear me so traduced," Hudson marveled. "But on the Sabbath at least I can think of other things."

"Miss Watters suggests I take the reading next Sunday, Mr. Hudson," Alistair said. "Have you already booked Fellows for the job, or will it be worth my while to speak to Dr. Everett?"

"Miss Watters suggested it, did she?" Hudson asked, casting an accusing glance at Lillian. "Are you changing horses in mid-stream, ma'am? A dangerous stunt. I see I must get busy and whip you into line." Then he turned to Alistair and added, "Fellows is booked for the duration."

"It is clear neither of you has a thought for politics on this day of rest," Lillian said ironically.

"Have you caught any more potatoes?" Sara asked Alistair, and he began a private flirtation with her, leaving Lillian free to monopolize Mr. Hudson.

"What a low trick to play," Hudson said to her.

"You will empty every pew in the church if you have Fellows reading to us all month."

"I don't refer to that particular low trick, but to your other one of setting up a flirtation with Sara's beau. I do occasionally give a thought to something beyond politics you know."

"Was it not politics you were discussing with Miss Ratchett just now?" she asked.

"Offense is the best defense. Is that it? Very well, I have set up a flirtation with Miss Ratchett, and if you forgive me, I shall forgive you. But I doubt Sara will be so lenient with you."

"I don't consider it a matter for forgiveness on either side."

"Not unforgivable, surely? You can't be so hardhearted as that."

"It has nothing to do with forgiveness. We are both free individuals and may flirt with whomever we like."

"*Whom*ever! What a schoolteacherish touch you give your broadmindedness," he said with a laugh. "Well, I am not so broadminded and take it very much amiss in you to be flirting with Alistair while my back is turned."

He was clearly not through using her yet, trying to jolly her along in this cunning manner. She sniffed and said, "You are wasting precious time, Mr. Hudson, and don't bother to pretend you aren't politicking, Sunday or no. There are the corn merchants without a soul whispering in their ears. Seven votes for you to toady up to."

He wrinkled a brow and frowned at her bad humor. "I'll get around to them. First things first. I have already twisted the arms and, I hope, votes of three merchants . . ."

"First things first!"

"Oh yes, I walked right into that one, didn't I? But in any case I feel all my recent efforts have earned me a reward. As I find you unoccupied, I would like to claim it now. I like to mix a little pleasure with my business when I can."

"I have noticed it."

"I hoped it might not escape your notice that I come to you as often as I can."

"Or to any halfway presentable female who is unattached. But I have no influence and no vote, so you can mix little business with the pleasure of speaking to me."

"It is the unalloyed pleasure of your conversation that attracts me. I come to bask myself in the glow of your insults and innuendo."

"With all the other women—you will notice I don't limit your coterie to ladies—puffing you up in your own conceit, you can well do with a little deflating."

"You have noticed how badly Mr. Saunders's hat fits my swollen head. But really, you know, the Baxter I brought with me still fits to a T."

"The swelling had set in before you got to Crockett then."

"Never at a loss for a quick set-down. Poor Fellows could do with some of your wit."

"He seems to be doing pretty well with yours. Alistair says he is doing better than they expected in any case."

"He'll make a fair puppet once we get him to London. His memory is not too bad."

Peeved that the conversation was turning again to politics, Lillian turned on him in some anger. "How can you in conscience put such a man up for office?"

"I wouldn't have; he was chosen as the candidate before I arrived. Allingham and Basingstoke are the culprits. But the party can use a few compliant hacks; we don't want every man a philosopher. He'll do just as he's told."

"You try to give the impression he is intelligent—someone who will personally look after his constituents."

"Do you think I really fool anyone? I hope so. No one would vote for him if it ever got out he's an idiot. It was Henry Wotton who defined an ambassador as 'an honest man sent to lie abroad for the good of his country.' I think of myself as an ambassador from London, sent to Crockett to lie for the good of my party. And the party would be good for the country. Having some experience in rationalization yourself, I think you follow my sophistry?"

"I don't know how you sleep nights!" she said, shaking her head and half-smiling to denote forgiveness.

"I didn't know you cared, or I should have told you sooner. On my stomach, and you?"

She looked startled, and rushed in, "I didn't mean that!"

"Did you not? Well, I don't snore, if that's what you're thinking," he added, pretending to be perplexed.

She felt obliged to be incensed at this, and assumed a pretty good imitation of it. "There is your puppet with the corn merchants. You'd better run over and slip him a few clever lines or he'll be telling them he means to cut the price of corn to six or seven shillings a bushel."

He looked at Fellows in alarm. "Oh Lord, I must go. Such a brief ray of sunlight as I am allowed at these wretched meetings of ours! See you at your aunt's tea party tomorrow. Don't let Alistair turn you into a Tory."

Alistair turned aside, for this last was said in a loud voice as Hudson walked away, and Lillian was again back in the Tory group, neither pleased nor entirely displeased with the short talk. She became quite definitely displeased, however, when Martha told them on the way home that Mr. Fellows had particularly asked them to send a card for the tea party to the Ratchetts. She went on to say that it was Hudson who wanted them invited. As Hudson was now distinguished and rich and all the rest of it, Martha hadn't a word to say against it, but wrote up the card and had it posted off before ever they sat down to lunch.

The tea party was set for Monday afternoon, and that morning they were quite busy preparing for it. On a busy Monday it would be mostly ladies who were free to attend, with a few elderly retired males.

Miss Ratchett, the last invited, was amongst the first arrivals, for she had been trying to scrape an acquaintance with the ladies at New Moon for some time. Lillian didn't have to be urged to make herself known to the girl, for she was highly eager to get a closer look at her. She was as elegant and pretty close-up as she appeared from afar. Her skin was clear, her eyes were bright, and other than a set of teeth small and sharp like a cat's, there was nothing amiss in her looks. Miss Ratchett proved to be an enthusiastic talker—and her talk was all of Mr. Hudson. He was "smart" and "elegant" and "a real gentleman." Her own elegance proved to be merely physical. Her opinions and speech were common in the extreme. This was a great relief to Miss Watters.

"I never saw such a smart gentleman since I left London," the girl told Lillian. "So clever and witty. He told me I was wasted in Crockett and should be in the City. I'm sure I've told Papa a hundred times we never should have moved out to the sticks, for how is a lady to find a decent *partie* in Crockett. Till Mr. Hudson came there wasn't a smart gentleman in the whole town, and he isn't planning to stay on after the election is over. There's Mr. Alistair, but he's so top-lofty there's no bearing it, and now he's dangling after Miss Monteith he's as good as caught. She's an elegant girl, don't you think, Miss Watters?"

"Yes, I like my cousin very much."

"Oh, she's your cousin. I wondered what you were doing here. Mr. Hudson never told me that. He mentioned New Moon a dozen times, but he never said you and Miss Monteith was cousins. He's coming to dinner, Mr. Hudson."

"Is he indeed?"

"We've sent all the way to Bristol for Westphalian ham, and hired two extra boys to serve table. I wanted Papa to serve champagne through the whole meal, but Mama says it's nouveau riche. Well, better nouveau than never, says I! Did you ever see such a quiz as that Mr. Fellows? A regular Bartholomew Baby, but he can certainly talk a blue streak. If he's the best man the Whigs can put forward they shouldn't bother running anyone, my papa says. And I told Mr. Hudson too, for he's the kind of a gentleman can take a joke. Mr. Hudson says Mr. Fellows is smarter than he looks, but then, he couldn't be dumber, could he? And they're saying around town it's even money he'll get in. I told Mr. Hudson if he gets in it's uneven money that will do it, for he's spending a shocking amount."

"Both parties are spending a good deal of money, I believe," Lillian said. Her relief at their guest's vulgarity was not total relief. She was vulgar, but also lively and amusing, and really Mr. Hudson did not appear in the least particular regarding vulgarity.

"I see you have a piano here. We have one too. I'm taking lessons from Miss Thistle. What a dowd she is! She wears the same dress every week. Look—there's Fellows and Hudson just come in now. My, he certainly is a smart-looking gentleman. Look at that, he's even speaking to the Floods. Whatever made your aunt ask them? They haven't even got a gig or a pony to their name."

Lillian was happy enough to escape the chatterbox, and went to greet the guest of honor. "By Jove, this is a bang-up do, Miss Watters. I could do with a cup of tea and a cake. We ate at the Cat's Paw again—a wonderful meal."

"The meat tough?" Lillian inquired politely.

"We had a brace of pigeons. Tainted, I fear. I felt sick as a dog, but Matthew says it was the third slice of plum cake that caused it. Daresay he's right. A clever fellow. I'll just bob along and make a few bows as Hudson told me to."

Hudson had already made his bows to Lady Monteith and Martha and was circulating amongst the crowd, smiling, complimenting, looking like a diplomat with his ceremonial bearing, and leaving behind him a row of smiles and blushes that told a truer story of the sort of conversation he was making than his appearance suggested. Miss Watters was keeping a sharp eye on him, as was Miss Ratchett.

Lillian noticed with joy that he had not distinguished the girl with any gallantry. She heard him discuss with apparent interest Mr. Pughe's gout and Miss Bellows's trouble with preserves going bad on her. Mr. Porter's cat was good for five minutes, its problem being that its hair was gone loose in its old age, and the poor thing was swallowing such a lot of it when grooming herself that she was getting colic. He recommended a dab of grease or oil for the condition, and moved on to the next vote.

Lillian was pouring tea to relieve Lady Monteith, who disliked pouring as it slowed down her own intake of cook's lovely macaroons and petits-fours. Three-quarters of an hour passed before Matthew strolled up to her with his cup empty.

"Good afternoon," he said. "What are you doing with yourself these days?"

"I'm surprised you find it necessary to ask. We have all been working hard for you getting this stupid tea party ready—and not one single man at it."

"On behalf of Mr. Fellows and myself, I must take exception to that statement. We are both single men."

"Not a single vote is what I meant. And pray don't bother to point out that Mr. Fellows has a vote. I trust that even he will know enough to vote for himself when it comes time to cast his ballot."

"I don't think I need tell him that, but I will, now that you mention it, just to be sure. But you underestimate the value of your party. We have had six invitations to call and three to dinner. There's a possible nine votes."

"A possible nine new flirts for you as well."

"Ten. The Whitlocks have no girls, but the Humbers and Dalmys have two each."

"It is not just the votes you are tallying up, I see."

"I have many interests, not least among them being attractive young ladies." He accepted his filled cup with a smile, but his eyes were soon roving around the room, and before long they had settled on Miss Ratchett. "I see you succeeded in getting Miss Ratchett here."

"Yes, as you most particularly requested it."

"She's an attractive girl, and her papa's pretty well in-laid, you know."

"A very wealthy merchant, I am given to understand. And she an only child too. Is marrying a fortune another of your varied interests?"

Hudson narrowed his eyes and looked prepared to be angry, but then smiled instead. "Not nice, Miss Watters. Upbraid me for my political machinations as much as you please and I shall endeavor to accept it with good grace, but don't, please, cast aspersions on my personal conduct or I shall take it amiss. I keep the two quite distinct."

"It seems to me you have mentioned mixing business and pleasure."

"Oh yes, but not business and romance, and certainly not business and marriage."

She looked at him closely, trying to figure out what he was saying, for he was regarding her as if he meant her to read some significance into the remark. "You recall we used the word 'flirtation' in connection with the young lady. With Miss Ratchett and her father it is business *and* pleasure, but not romance.

This was agreeable news, but Lillian had already gone on ahead of him, trying to figure out the nature of his connection with herself. The word flirtation had not been used, but certainly he had been flirting with her.

"Now don't frown at me, please. You know we can only ever meet for minutes at a time. Let us not waste our precious minutes in quarreling," he said.

"We're not quarreling," she answered, shocked at the tender tone of his voice and the look he was giving her. If this was flirting, it went a good deal beyond anything Lillian had been involved in before, and she had had more than one flirt in her twenty-one years.

"Good!" he said heartily. "We'll quarrel as much as you like after this election is over, but for the present getting Tony elected is a big-enough problem for me. I don't want to have to worry about having hurt your feelings, too. Have I? You seem awfully quiet and have been noticeably bad-tempered of late."

"No, no. My feelings are not so sensitive as that."

"I think they are, but I didn't mean to rip up at you. Perhaps I'm more sensitive myself than this cowhide veneer I wear would suggest. Miss Ratchett does not misunderstand the matter, you know. I am not making up to her in any way that could possibly suggest to her a serious attachment. It is hardly even a flirtation."

Lillian could accept that this was true, at least practically speaking, for Miss Ratchett had already said that Mr. Hudson had no intention of remaining in town. But why Hudson should be telling her was not at all clear. "I didn't accuse you of leading her on," she said, hardly knowing what reply to make him, but clearly he was waiting for some exculpation.

"Then we are still friends?"

"Yes, certainly." She was becoming more lost by the moment.

"Good. How about a ray of sunlight before I go, then? A smile—just a little one?" he asked, smiling himself. She laughed in confusion. "That's better. You have a lovely smile, you know. Notice that I don't suggest you use it to buy us votes. And especially don't feel required to use it on Alistair!"

After this enchanting piece of flirtation, he turned and walked straight over to Miss Ratchett, to spend a near-fifteen minutes with her in apparent delight that gave a strong hint of romance, whatever he might say to the contrary. And he had not spent five minutes with herself. Then he would go home and change his clothing . . . to dine with the Ratchetts! He received no more of Lillian's sunlight that afternoon, and after he had left his speech and behavior were subjected to a scrutiny that would have astonished him had he been aware of it. Lillian vehemently deemed him an utterly treacherous man. He would say or do anything to gain his ends, and if he thought he would receive no more quarrels from her, he was badly mistaken.

*9*

❧❧❧❧❧❧❧❧❧❧❧❧❧❧❧❧❧❧❧❧❧❧❧❧❧❧❧❧❧❧❧❧❧❧❧❧

THE harvest ball, ostensibly arranged by Basingstoke and his friends, was much discussed and looked forward to in Crockett. It was to be something different from any party ever thrown before. Some genteel families assumed that the price of a guinea a couple would keep out the riff-raff, but it was not the organizers' wish that anyone with a vote be excluded, so they gave away more tickets than they sold. The dinner preceding the ball, however, was limited by the size of the hall to one hundred persons, and it promised to be a more decorous do than the dancing afterward.

On the arranged evening, Fellows and Hudson called for the ladies of New Moon and the six proceeded to the Assembly Hall, where the one hundred of Crockett society were gathering, the gentlemen in their black jackets and pantaloons, the costume chosen by the whipper-in who did not wish to put the local worthies to the expense of satin breeches they would not be likely to require again in their lives. The ladies, however, had no limits placed on how grand an ensemble they might devise. There were satins, silks and laces enough to equal the greatest ton party in London. Nine-tenths of the jewels might be paste and the pearls coated with fish scales, but in the candlelight they sparkled and glowed as well as genuine jewels, and gave the wearers as much pleasure.

Fellows had Sara on one arm and her mother on the other, while Hudson escorted Lillian and her Aunt Martha. Alistair and his whipper-in were present, for no overt political overtones were to be acknowledged. In fact Hudson had given him two tickets, for it seemed ungentlemanly to force them to contribute a guinea to the Whig cause. These matters were understood to a nicety between them.

Alistair accosted Fellows's party as soon as they entered and made himself pleasant to them all. It was only Sara who showed any joy at this circumstance. She detached herself from Fellows with such unexpected alacrity that no one had time to pull her back into the fold.

"Has anyone else been throwing potatoes at you, Mr. Alistair?" she asked eagerly. Having the keenest interest in the campaign, about the only fact she had discovered for a week was that people threw potatoes at Mr. Alistair, and she thought it very mean of them.

"No, no, I am not so unpopular as that," he assured her.

"Indeed you are not! I'm sure you must be the most popular gentleman in the parish."

"I hope I am the most popular in the constituency, in any case."

"There too. I am sure no one else looks half so well in evening clothes."

The lady was so beautiful and so admiring that Alistair was much of a mind to remain at her side, leaving Reising alone to politick for the party. All through the two glasses of sherry preceding the meal, she inveighed against people who threw potatoes, till finally Mr. Hudson went after her himself and tucked her arm in his, to lead her to the table. Mr. Fellows was too well occupied gossiping with Allingham and Basingstoke to notice her defection, or to think he was wasting his own time preaching to the converted. Indeed he was not preaching at all, but hearing with dismay from Mr. Basingstoke that he had been thrown over by his flirt, Lady Marie Sinclair, with whom he had long been waging a campaign.

"She has given me my *congé*, Mr. Fellows," Basingstoke said. "I lay the fault at your door. It was you and Hudson barging in at Ashley Hall that aroused Sir John's suspicions. I don't believe he had tumbled to it at all till you went there."

"I wonder Hudson did it, for he is generally pretty surefooted in these matters," Fellows said.

"Well, he ain't infallible, I suppose."

With no notion what the word meant, and no dictionary to aid him, Fellows replied only obliquely. "The devil you say, Mr. Basingstoke. Well, unlucky in love, lucky in war, what?"

Mr. Basingstoke did not immediately grasp the import of words, but Fellows explained, "The election, I mean. Lucky in the election."

"Oh, aye, the election—there was the *casus belli* between us."

Fellows hung on his every unintelligible word, hoping subsequent talk would reveal their obscurity to him. "Aye, the cause of the war between us was politics," Basingstoke went on. "Sir John, her good man, is a Tory, and I am *persona non grata* at Ashley Hall."

*Persona non grata* was a phrase well-known to Fellows, from being so often one himself, but he did not quite grasp the other foreign phrase and was eager to do so. "So you and Lady Marie are at *casus belli,* are you?" he ventured.

"Politics—there's your *casus belli,* but I daresay after the campaign is over she'll let me back in. *Amor omnia vincit,* you know."

"Just what I say myself, old chap." What a clever devil he was, to be sure. Always a new twist to him. "So it's au revoir to Lady Marie till after the *casus belli,* I take it?" Fellows asked, feeling that he had at last translated the phrase accurately.

"Au revoir and adieu, auf Wiedersehen and adios."

"By Jove!" Fellows gasped, marveling at this longheaded wizard with the power of so many tongues.

Lillian and Martha were presented to this font of wisdom and were as struck by his words as Fellows, but in the opposite way. They were aghast to see that the "longheaded Basingstoke" was none other than a foolish, dumpy squire, cast in much the same mold as Fellows himself and respected only because he had got to university and peppered his speech with foreign phrases.

At dinner, Alistair sat across the table from Sara, and they spent so much time looking and smiling at each other that neither overheard a word of Mr. Fellows's multilingual table-talk, in which *casus belli*'s and *sine qua non*'s jostled with *caveat emptor*'s in terrible confusion.

Mr. Hudson supposed there might possibly have been an hour in his career that equaled this one for sheer horror, but he could not put a finger on it. Between Sara cozying up to the Tory—and she was so lovely that she was much regarded despite her stupidity—and Mr. Fellows making an ass of himself, he was on tenterhooks from soup till sweet. Fellows inveighed against every morsel of food he ate, and he consumed a good many tasty morsels. He spoke in a loud voice down the table to Mr. Basingstoke, letting the locals know he had tasted better fish and fowl elsewhere, in London to be precise. And every bite of it made and donated by his voters' wives! A silent glare from Hudson reminded him of his duty and he added punctiliously, "Of course, it's very fine for such bad food." Some minor irritation was added to Mr. Hudson's vexation by the fact that Miss Watters was on her high ropes for some reason, and after he had been at such pains to talk her down from them, too. He might have had some small pleasure from Tony's million faux pas if she had shared a smile with him, but she was cool to the point of freezing. Sara sat on his right and received the greater part of his attention to distract her from Mr. Alistair, and on those few occasions when he dared to direct a look or a word to Lillian, she looked at him as though he were a cup or a saucer, or better a dirty dish.

Lillian too thought it an abominable meal, with Mr.

Hudson showing Sara the distinction of taking her to table and honoring her with nine-tenths of his time. This, coming on top of his *à suivie* flirtation with Miss Ratchett, in whose direction he was still smiling at intervals during the meal, galled her mightily. To add to her annoyance, she couldn't get Mr. Alistair to so much as look at her in order to make Hudson jealous. When at last the meal was over and she stood with Sara waiting for a partner, Hudson walked purposefully toward them. Her heart lifted despite his treachery. At least he was going to dance with her first!

"Will you get a hand on Fellows?" he asked her, and then turned to Sara to ask her to stand up with himself.

She was through with hopping through hoops for him! She wouldn't have stood up with Fellows if he'd gone down on his knees and begged her. When Mr. Alistair, also coming for Sara but having her whisked off under his nose, asked her to stand up with him, she accepted with the greatest good will and exerted herself to the utmost to keep him well entertained, that Mr. Hudson might see she was not a despicable partner. She noticed with anger that Miss Ratchett, in an expensive, gorgeous, and much too fancy rose silk gown, was the next young lady to have Mr. Hudson's company. She herself had only the minimal pleasure of standing up with Mr. Basingstoke and hearing his polyglot talk, one half of which she could not understand, and two halves of which was not worth listening to in any case.

The evening wore on, becoming noisier and more crowded as those with free tickets came in. Lillian was sure Martha would whisk them off home and she had not had one dance with Mr. Hudson, nor said more than a word to him. But Martha had secured the company of

Lord Allingham and was not about to part with a lord merely because every vulgar hedgebird in town was rubbing elbows with her nieces. A title was a dearly beloved thing to Martha; she was busy substantiating details of Mr. Hudson's pending title and estates and trying to decide which of her nieces it was he merited.

Lillian's evening continued steadily downhill. She had to be jerked around the hall by Mr. Fellows for a waltz, and then was made to feel worse by seeing Mr. Hudson sink from Miss Ratchett to a brace of women who had all the earmarks of ladies of pleasure. Their garish, low-cut gowns, their loud laughter and their immodest ogling of every man in the room left little doubt as to their calling. She was pretty sure it was Hudson who had brought them in, along with his flash culls. Who else could be so low? She was rapidly reaching the conclusion she should ask her aunt to take them home.

It was 11:30, nearing intermission, when she glanced up to see Mr. Hudson walking toward her group, with Fellows in tow. She turned resolutely away to ask Martha on the spot if they could go home.

"Go home? My dear, we'll wait just a little. Here is Mr. Fellows come to dance with you." As Hudson was favoring Sara this evening, Fellows was falling to Lillian's lot.

"Well, Miss Watters, it looks like I am stuck to stand up and jig it with you again," Fellows told her. "At least you are lightfooted—I'll say that for you thin girls—you ain't heavy to steer around the floor."

"A pity we can't say the same for you!" she retaliated, her anger suddenly too great to suppress. And he had to say it in front of Mr. Hudson too!

"By Jove, you've a sharp tongue in your head! But you

skinny girls are all alike. Sour as vinegar, every one of you."

"You haven't danced with me, Mr. Fellows," the artless Sara proclaimed, and Mr. Fellows was encouraged to turn his suave charms in her direction.

"He's in a bad skin because I've been giving him a rare raking-down," Hudson apologized to Miss Watters. "Was there ever such a night at this? I thought dinner would never be over, between *casus belli* and tainted fowl."

The words were fine, but Lillian could not quite forget that the appalling dinner had been over for several hours, and this was the first decent conversation she had had with him. "Bad-tempered, skinny girls have added nothing to the night, I daresay," she replied tartly.

"Nonsense, you're a fine figure of a woman," he answered rather unthinkingly, only wanting to placate her.

"Thank you very much." She was accustomed to hear herself complimented occasionally as a "pretty girl," and to have graduated overnight to a "fine figure of a woman" implied an advanced maturity with which she was not ready, in her greenish years, to come to terms.

"Did I say something gauche? I have been too much with the candidate. I mean it as a compliment."

"High praise indeed. Why not make it a portly dame and have done with it?"

"Not for another ten years. I have aged you with my poor praise, is that it? But you surely need no reassurance as to your appearance. You and your cousin are the fairest flowers in the room. It is hard to tell which is the more beautiful specimen."

"Most people have no trouble telling which is the more beautiful," she replied. "It is quite clear, I think."

He compared them judiciously. "You're right. You have

the definite edge, but it is unbecoming in you to say so yourself," he said with a smile.

"I didn't mean that! You know she is much prettier. In fact, it is no comparison at all. I am plain and I know it."

"Another bad trait—putting yourself down to worm more compliments out of me. But I'm not so stingy that you need resort to tricks. The fairest of them all, as usual."

"Don't be absurd," she answered, flustered at the flattery. "Everyone knows Sara is beautiful."

"Beauty lies in the eye of the beholder."

"You are indebted to Mr. Fellows for that striking truism, I assume. A pity he hadn't remembered comparisons are odious. When the beholder's eye becomes so purblind as yours seems to be, it is time he looked into a pair of spectacles."

"Or better, through them, but my eyes aren't that far gone yet. Oh, they blur out the crow's foot and the spots, no doubt."

"They must also deprive you of the sight of a dimple, must they not?"

"Have you a dimple, Miss Watters? You should try a smile once in a while to show it."

"We thin, sour females have no truck with smiles."

"Don't lay Fellows's compliments at my door. Vent your ill humor on him, if you are determined to be nasty. I came in peace and charity."

"You may keep your charity."

"But not, it seems, the peace. I perceive a frost setting in, and here it is only October."

"I'm surprised if you do perceive it. I hadn't thought

you were perceiving anything beyond the set of dashers you have brought in to liven up your little party."

He looked at her in a knowing way that infuriated her. "So that's it! Tell me, is it their presence or my attendance on them that has you in the boughs?"

"I am not in the boughs."

"I beg to differ. Right up there in the branches with the jays and crows and other bird-witted creatures."

"If you want the truth, then, I think it was a perfectly scandalous thing to do, bringing in loose females to—to influence men's voting."

"They would stare to hear you describe their activities so euphemistically."

"Yes—well, the less said about how they mean to do it, the better in polite company, but that is why they're here, isn't it?"

"Their main aim is to fill their pockets, and they will certainly do it in that manner too low to be mentioned in polite company. If they can swing a few votes in the process, well, that is only incidental."

"You should be ashamed of yourself. I'm ashamed for you."

"You owe me an apology, for once. I do draw the line at whoremongering, believe it or not. It was Reising who brought them in. There are limits to how low I will sink, even for the party."

"It is you who is chummying up to them. But perhaps it has nothing to do with politics."

"Wrong again! It has only to do with politics. Since they are here, I don't want them upsetting the applecart. This stunt does more harm than good. No man is going to be swayed to vote for anyone only on a—er—female's suggestion. I merely pointed out to them the Tories with the deepest pockets. Once they have frisked the squires of a pony or so and bolted back to London, I wonder whether their gents won't be eager to vote against the dashers' advice. Tell me now, do I reason wrongly?"

"Not you, Machiavelli!" she charged. "Never a wrong step."

"Why does that sound so awfully like an insult, I wonder?"

"I didn't mean it as a compliment."

"At least it is an old insult. If that is the worst you have to say of my conduct, or lack of it, I don't despair. We may see a little St. Martin's summer yet before the evening is out." He saw no signs of it in Miss Watters's direction, however, and commented to himself that despite his reputation, he seemed to have made some wrong step.

Miss Watters turned her head quite in the opposite direction, and there was a silence between them till the music struck up.

"Well, Beanpole," he said unceremoniously, "there is a waltz striking up and you've let Sara walk away with Fellows right under your nose. You are stuck to jig with me. A fine dancer—only two left feet, of course, and no sense of rhythm."

"If you're sure the London molls can spare you," she answered, cajoled into a brief smile.

"Oh, I didn't dance with them. I am too top-lofty for that. Just gave 'em a little advice to make sure they didn't go interfering with my Whigs." He led her to the floor, where his two left feet contrived rather well to follow the music. "Why didn't you dance with Fellows when I asked you to?" he inquired.

"You didn't ask me, you *told* me. I am not in your employ, like the flash culls."

"I would have been happy to pay you," he said, smiling and refusing to take offense at her continuing pique. "You know how free I make with other people's money. You might have earned yourself a good sum. Why should the dashers be the only ones to profit from this little shindig?"

"There isn't enough money in all the Whig coffers to make me go along with your stunts."

"You have gone along with them without a penny till now. Has Alistair perverted your reason? Are you turning Tory on me? I noticed you two laughing it up. Bad enough he has snatched Sara on us; don't you succumb to his blandishments too.'

"Till after the election, you mean."

"Not *ever* I mean, Sourpuss."

"I think you should limit the number of your flirtations, Mr. Hudson. Not even you, with all your light-fingered skills, can juggle so many of us at one time."

"Bungled, have I?" he asked humbly. "I hope I have not dropped the important ball."

"Miss Ratchett seems to be in good spirits still," she assured him.

"I never thought you'd be the jealous type," he answered, remaining unoffended. She felt a perfect fool to be made to feel jealous by a man who had not distinguished her by any more attention than he had shown to other girls in the community.

"I have nothing to be jealous of."

"I am glad you realize it," he told her, his dulcet tone removing any ambiguity from the words. The look that accompanied this speech confirmed his meaning.

"As if I would be jealous of a man who came here to bribe and corrupt and tear down barn doors and flirt with —with dashers!"

"And rich Cit's daughters. Don't leave out Miss Ratchett. I have a notion she is offense number one. Dare I suggest even the *casus belli* between us? The very *sine qua non* of our little misunderstanding, for I refuse to believe you are foolish enough to be jealous of dashers. But Tony's latest scholarly acquisition—and it will be my last detour into Latin, I promise you—gives me some hope. *Amor omnia vincit.*"

"I don't understand Latin," she said a little mendaciously, for she knew at least this phrase well enough.

"I won't bore you with a translation. I have an idea you're determined not to understand English tonight either, as spoken by me. Well, it is a great pity, for there was something I was particularly looking forward to telling you."

"What is it?" she asked, curious and also somewhat mollified by his cajolery.

"Oh no, I don't mean to reward you for all your hard words, Miss Watters. I have learned not to practice my bribery and corruption on *you*. Let us by all means keep pure Watters pure. You must wait and read it in the papers tomorrow, like everyone else."

"But what is it?"

"Try a little bribery of your own. You well know I'm corruptible. Very."

"What do you mean?"

"Think about it," he said teasingly, and laughed. "What would a pretty young girl—or even a fine figure of a woman—use to bribe a man?"

"Money, of course," she answered with a studied obtuseness.

"Just for that, I really won't tell you. I can be a stubborn oaf too," he said, and refused to be talked around.

The dance was over too soon, and Miss Watters was at too high a tide of jealousy to put forth her best efforts at bribery, and so she never found out. She knew perfectly well Mr. Hudson was making fun of her, the more so as he went directly from her to Miss Ratchett and sent her a mocking smile across the room. He was obviously an incorrigible flirt, and she an irreclaimable idiot to lose as much as a minute's composure over him. For the remaining quarter of an hour allowed her at the dance she didn't look at a soul but Mr. Alistair, causing Sara to think her cousin was not really so nice as she had come to imagine. The party had reached such a rowdy level by this time that even the presence of Lord Allingham could not induce Martha to remain. There was some little confabulation then, as it was not desirable for the ladies' escorts to leave the field to the Tories, yet they must have one gentleman, at least, to see them home.

A successful solution was for Lord Allingham to take them, and with unhappy hearts Sara and Lillian were taken away, leaving behind Mr. Alistair and Mr. Hudson to make up to all the fortunate females (including Miss Ratchett), who were not too high-born to stay at such a wild frolic as the harvest ball was becoming.

## 10

M<small>ISS</small> Martha Monteith slept ill the night after the ball. Having learned from Lord Allingham that Mr. Hudson was not only heir to a barony, but a very rich gentleman in his own right, as well as a man of huge consequence in the party, she lay awake for two hours trying to decide what to do with him. It seemed to her he had shown a marked preference for Sara's company, taking her to dinner and standing up first with her. On the other hand, there was Mr. Fellows residing so wonderfully close to New Moon. It would be very handy for Melanie to have Sara married on her own doorstep. Then, too, there was the little detail of Sara being a fool, whereas Mr. Hudson was a clever man who might possibly require a sharp wife to help him in his party doings. That pointed to Lillian, but there back in Yorkshire was Mr. Thorstein and his fine estate, his fortune, and his shelves full of lovely woolen goods.

It was a new problem to have too many beaux to go around, and she dickered with herself as to which of them was expendable. She passed over Mr. Alistair entirely— not that she had failed to observe his interest in Sara, she wasn't that blind—but only because four beaux for two girls was too much. His being a Tory would not in the normal way have been any impediment, but in the midst of a heated-up campaign it served as an excuse to eliminate him and get the number down to manageable proportions. The problem was still unresolved when she arose in the morning in a cross mood as a result of her lack of sleep.

Martha had a chance to gauge Mr. Hudson's preference in the matter of a bride very soon after arising, for he had relented during the past hours and decided to inform his cohorts of his news before it was made public in the papers. He and Fellows came to call on their way to the village.

"We are just on our way to Crockett to meet Mr. Telford," Mr. Fellows told the four ladies.

"Indeed, and who might Mr. Telford be?" Martha inquired eagerly, wondering if she had yet another possible husband to dispose of.

"He builds canals," Fellows told her.

"And bridges, Tony," Hudson reminded him.

"Has it to do with a bridge for the river?" Lillian asked.

"Yes, by Jove. If those Tories think to keep all the treats for their own ridings, Matt and I will have Telford throw a bridge across the Severn for us Whigs to use."

It was necessary for Mr. Hudson to explain the nature of the plan. "The Tories promise a bridge every election, but they have not delivered it yet, and there is no reason to think they will do so this time. We have been in touch with Mr. Telford, a marvelous engineer who has constructed many canals and harbors and bridges, and have got him interested in trying out a new sort of bridge that was erected in America fifteen years ago. It's called a suspension bridge. Towers are built on either side of the river. Chains are laid across with hanger-rods suspending, and a roadway is held by the rods. It sounds precarious enough, but it is a very solid sort of construction, actually, if it is engineered properly, and Telford is the best."

"It sounds awfully risky," Sara said, picturing a road swaying in the breeze suspended from a couple of chains.

"It is a novel and very ingenious idea, I think," Hudson told her. "Telford is very excited about it."

"Who will pay for it?" Martha asked.

"The people who use it," Hudson replied.

"Mr. Hudson, you cannot think that will get you any votes," Lillian said feelingly. "The cost would be enormous. You'll lose even your Whig votes if you go ahead with this."

"Already told you, *I* ain't paying a penny!" Fellows reminded him with a wounded countenance. "Dipped into my own pocket to the tune of five hundred pounds already. Had no notion it was so dear to become an M.P."

"How will it be financed, exactly?" Martha asked.

"The money has been raised locally from wealthy citizens. The cost is not so great as you might think, for Telford is mainly interested in the welfare of the people and in trying a new technique, so he doesn't look to make much profit from it. The incentive for the builders to use their own money is that it is a private bridge—they have bought the land on either side of the river where the bridge will begin and end, and they will charge a toll for using it."

"The Tories wouldn't make us pay no toll," Fellows grouched.

"The toll will only be levied on carriages and perhaps mounted riders. We haven't worked out all the details, but foot-passengers—the poor, in other words—will not be required to pay. The revenue will come out of the pockets of those who can well afford it, and they won't all be local people by any means. Over the years the cost will be paid off, and it will provide a good return on the investment of the builders. It is bound to lead to an improvement in the roads with the traffic it will bring, but the Tories can foot the bill for that."

"Who are these local citizens who have funded it?" Martha inquired.

"Mr. Ratchett is the major investor," Mr. Hudson replied, with a quizzing look at Lillian. "I have had a good deal of business with him lately. He has so much money he doesn't know what to do with it."

"He could give me a little for my campaign," Tony muttered to himself.

"He did give us a hundred pounds," Hudson said.

"Allingham is in on it, and I am myself. I am not a local citizen, of course, but as I sponsored the idea and Tony was reluctant to put his own money up, I thought it would secure confidence in the project and encourage others to join in. I think it will prove to be a good investment. I do not consider it money wasted by any means. And it will be good for the town; a new project of this sort will bring plenty of business. And it would be the first suspension bridge in England. It will put Crockett on the map."

"And it's us Whigs that did it," Fellows declared, after having fought the project tooth and nail every step of the way.

"That's right, Tony," Hudson said. "Don't forget that point. The Tories have promised a bridge forever, but it's a Whig who got it. And remember, there is no toll for foot-passengers, whereas they must pay a couple of pennies now to be taken across by the boatman."

"Yessir, and if they don't vote for me, I might not have Telford go ahead with it," Fellows added.

"The deal is signed," Hudson reminded him, but this made no impression on Tony.

"Nossir, I just might not let them have it."

An announcement of such significance had to be talked over for several minutes, during which time coffee was prepared and served.

"It will be fine to have a bridge," Lady Monteith declared. "I do hate taking the barge to Chepstow, and the stores are very fine there." Her social duty done, she settled back with her coffee and sweet bun.

"Does Mr. Alistair know?" Sara asked.

"Not yet. We hope to catch him off guard," Hudson told her. Throwing a bridge at him seemed a trick more cruel even than throwing potatoes, and Sara soon vanished mysteriously from the room. Closeted in her own, she wrote up the information in a note and sent it off to Alistair, who received it that evening, several hours after he had heard the awful news in the village. But he thought it very nice of her to have warned him.

Martha felt that some particular marks of condescension toward Mr. Hudson were in line now that she knew more about him, and she bestowed them in a catechism of impertinent questions regarding his parentage, his titled uncle, his estates real and to come, his work in the party, and his freedom. "And you are not engaged or anything of that sort?" she ended up, making the point of her questions so obvious that Lillian writhed in embarrassment. Hudson took it all in seeming stoicism, betraying not a glimmer of the resentment Lillian was sure he must be feeling. Martha was so cheered by what she heard from him that she dashed off upstairs at once to fetch Sara down, so as to allow Hudson to decide which of the two girls he wanted. It was a rare privilege that she was thus allowing him: to make his own choice.

"Do you think I passed?" Hudson said to Lillian with a twinkling smile when Martha left the room.

"Auntie is always curious about everyone," she explained.

"I will be happy to refer her to my man of business if there are any details she forgot to ask," he said, obviously undeceived by this excuse. "And I think Allingham will give me a character reference."

"You have managed to stay pretty well out of his way, have you?"

"No, but I lied a lot to him."

Lady Monteith overheard this last remark and frowned at Mr. Hudson. Fellows, bored with such a small audience, none of whom was paying the least heed to himself, turned to Lady Monteith.

"You are a friend of Lady Marie Sinclair, I think, ma'am?"

"Yes, I have known her forever."

"Do you see much of her?"

"No, she lives three miles away, you know, and I seldom see her, except once in a while in Crockett."

"That's a pity then."

Lady Monteith was not overly curious, but inquired, after another bite of sweet bun, "Why?"

"Had a falling out with Basingstoke. Pity. He's all cut up about it."

Hudson, overhearing this, was swift to object. "You won't want to involve yourself in anything of this sort, Tony. She is a married lady and a Tory to boot, remember. We have already stumbled in on them once and been hinted away. Don't get mixed up in other people's marital problems."

"She may be a Tory, but she's a devilish fine-looking woman for all that. Blond hair and blue eyes—or brown. Eyes, anyway, very nice ones."

"Only a squint and a little cross-eyed," Lillian said in a low tone to Mr. Hudson.

He was cheered to find her coming out of her sulks. "A fine figure, too—as broad as a barn door."

"I see what your compliment to me last night was worth. I too was a fine figure of a woman, and me skinny as a pole!"

"It's you who should be tucking into that plateful of cream buns. Shall I get you one before your aunt gobbles them all up?"

She shook her head, smiling. "This bridge you speak of, will it make a big difference in the campaign?"

"I think it will shift the balance. If only we could corner a handful of the grain-growers' votes, we might rest easy. We have one last do coming up—a dinner for the veterans, and several of them are farmers' sons. If we could come up with some trick for that, it would be a help. It is quite shameful the way the government is treating the veterans —no work for them, and if the disabled are getting any pension, it is small and irregular. Reising has the advantage in the affair, as it is the Tories who are in power, and he can bring in Castlereagh or Eldon or some other name to impress the locals, to shake hands with Alistair, and lend him a quite false air of being somebody."

"Have you no Whig name you could bring in?"

"Some of the dukes are Whigs, but they wouldn't put themselves to the bother of going out on the hustings. Couldn't bear to tear themselves away from their mistresses."

"You should let them know what dashing lightskirts abound in Crockett since you two whippers-in are come to town."

"It is only one whipper-in who brought lightskirts!"

"Yes, the other sanctimonious gentleman was content with pickpockets and cat-throwers and making up to the Tory lightskirts."

"The girls are apolitical. Like your friend Alistair, till they are branded I consider them fair game. Well, we have Brougham and Tierney who might impress a cityful of university graduates, but I doubt they'd cut much ice in Crockett. What we require is a hero. A pity Lord Byron wouldn't come. He's a Whig when he's not busy being a lover or a poet or posing for a picture."

"It's not a literary community. A war hero would be better, particularly as it is veterans you want to impress. Wellington, I think, is a Tory, though."

"Oh God, don't let Reising get that idea! That's all we need, to have the Iron Duke here campaigning against us." He sat silent a moment, thinking, then a smile lightened his face. "But Wellington didn't win the war quite singlehanded, despite his boasts to that effect. There is Colonel Dorking, a good friend of mine, who lost a leg at Salamanca—a chestful of ribbons and a dashing scarlet tunic. I think you've given me an inspiration, Lily."

"Lily!"

"This is no time to quibble about my manners. I must dash a note off to Dorking. And we've got to get to the village to meet Telford too. Where the devil has everyone gone? We should take our leave of your Aunt Martha."

Martha entered just then with Sara at her heels, in time to say good-bye to the gentlemen and then castigate her young niece as a peagoose as soon as they were gone, to have missed such a chance to nab a husband.

The villagers were in awe to be the recipients of a stunning new bridge of a sort never before seen in England. The merchants foresaw much increase in business and prices; the innkeeper, a good profit from rooms rented and meals provided; the foot-passengers, many a pleasant free walk across the water to Chepstow. It proved an additional advantage that the Tories had so long promised a bridge and not fulfilled their promise.

Reising made what he could of its being a toll bridge, but he knew he had sustained a severe, perhaps killing, blow, and he set his mind to work to counterattack. His main contributor of funds, Sir John Sinclair, was unhappy with him. He was miffed at Hudson's going to Ashley

Hall and at Fellows's dangling after Lady Marie. Strange that Hudson had stood still for that. If worse came to worst, he would put the screws to Sir John, but he didn't see that things could get much worse. However, there was still the veterans' dinner.

Telford was paraded about town and soon was being called by his old nickname of Laughing Tàm by the townsfolk, who took to his winning ways very well and listened with interest to his stories about building the Ellesmere Canal and the Caledonian Canal in Scotland. Not one to waste time, Telford was soon seen on the site, with surveyors and other interesting persons performing tasks whose purpose could only be imagined. A sketch of the bridge was drawn up and put on display in the newspaper office window, where it received a good deal of attention. It was to be known as the Fellows Bridge, at least till after the election, when it might very well become the Ratchett Bridge, or the Allingham Bridge. Even the corn-growers had to admit it would be a help in getting their produce to the northern markets of York and Northumberland.

Many an afternoon Mr. Fellows and Hudson were to be seen clambering down the banks of the Severn River with a group of interested spectators trailing at their heels, being informed by Mr. Fellows that it was the first bridge of its kind ever built. When a cautious man dared to ask whether it would be safe—the first of its kind and so revolutionary—he was told they had one just like it in America, and it was safe as a church, so where was the danger in it?

The bridge site was fast becoming a general meeting place, so it was only natural that Miss Ratchett go to see what her papa was spending his blunt on. Natural, too, that she should be received with special respect by Mr. Hudson and Fellows. It became her custom to lure the former up from the banks to walk her home as often as she could. The ladies of New Moon also made more than one trip to the bridge site, and Aunt Martha was considerably distressed to see the heir of a barony debased through falling into common Cit hands.

She found Miss Ratchett "forthcoming," as she phrased it, and urged her own nieces to follow her example and put themselves a little forward. Her words fell on deaf ears. Sara was convinced the bridge would sway dreadfully, hung up by only a couple of little chains, and swore she would never set foot on it. She grew ill just thinking of it, and had no generosity toward its instigators. It was very bad of Mr. Fellows and Hudson to foist such a dangerous contraption on them, and she told Mr. Alistair so every time she saw him. Potatoes were forgotten entirely. He heartily agreed with her in his replies, but in truth he was fascinated by the bridge—Whig bridge though it would be. With a bent for engineering, he was intrigued by the project, and became one of Telford's most ardent fans, to the chagrin of Reising.

Miss Watters said not a word against the bridge, but when she saw Mr. Hudson leading Miss Ratchett up the bank several days in a row, she came to hate it as thoroughly as did Sara. She made no effort to engage Hudson's attention, and in fact refused to see him when he waved. Martha was at her wits' end with her two unmarried nieces and began to speak of sending Lillian home to snap up Mr. Thorstein before she lost him to some Cit's chit too.

"Appropriate, Aunt Martha. He's a Cit himself," Lillian reminded her.

"Yes, you may look down your nose at him, but I don't see you lift a finger to get Cecilford's heir." Hudson had become Cecilford's heir in Martha's repinings, to remind the girls of the glory awaiting them if only they would get cracking.

It was assumed as a matter of course, by Mr. Reising and Mr. Alistair, that Mr. Telford would be the Whigs' speaker at the dinner for the veterans. They had got Lord Bathurst to come down to speak for them and shake Alistair's hand before the town, but they felt that even the Minister of War and the Colonies might not outshine Laughing Tam, particularly as the village was now alive with workmen and newspapermen and all sorts of revenue-producing people. The bridge had become the most-discussed subject in town, and it was invariably spoken of as the Fellows Bridge, thus putting forward the Whig candidate. Reising began to see that he would have to sink to a stunt that even he did not consider perfectly fair, and drove the ten miles to have discussions with Sir John.

*11*

Iᴛ came as a severe blow to Reising and Alistair that a Colonel Dorking had been sneaked into town and hidden out at St. Christopher's Abbey, to be sprung on them at the Veterans' Dinner in full regimentals, complete with wooden leg, cane, and medals. Bathurst hadn't a chance against him. All he could do was boast of the victory at Waterloo in terms of quite dull statistics, with an emphasis on the cost in terms of pounds and pence. He had seen the war from behind a desk at Whitehall, and had nothing to say of interest to veterans.

Dorking had been there, in the middle of all the blood and thunder—had left a leg there for his country. He was a tall, soft-spoken gentleman whose manner went down well after the bombast of Bathurst. He spoke in eloquent terms of the bravery of the soldiers, mentioning by name and regiment the two boys lost by Crockett. He knew what battles they had been in, and what battle had killed them. He knew too, as a soldier, the importance of those battles, and could assure the parents and other listeners that the young men had not died in vain.

The townspeople knew all about the boys' records, but they heard it as though for the first time, for they only knew it from letters and papers, and here was a voice from across the water, telling it as it actually was. More than one tear was surreptitiously wiped away, and it was an all-male audience. Dorking had them in the palm of his hand, and when he made the subtle shift from war to politics, he still had them. Nothing could be done for the dead, but was it not a shame—even a crime—that so little was done for those who had returned, and especially for those who returned mutilated? Not a glance down at his own missing leg at this point, but only a slight jiggle to remind them he stood propped up on a wooden leg. It was marvelously done; Hudson thought he should be on the stage.

From the general injustice, Dorking began moving to particular local items. Was it not the very least to be done for these brave boys who returned without an arm or a leg that they be given jobs of a sedentary nature when the government had them to give? But of course it was not the case. This was recognized by all the locals as a reference to the post office job having gone to Jed Evans, the late M.P.'s nephew, who was well able to earn his bread by the sweat of his brow, when Corporal Winton had applied for it. Corporal Winton sat blushing, taking care not to look at his sleeve, which was pinned to his jacket as it had no arm to fill it. It was a moving, emotional speech, and even the Tories present were made to feel there had been some nefarious doings in their town under Tory management.

It was not fair for the Whigs to have two speakers at the dinner and the Tories only one, so Mr. Telford's speech was given unofficially, from his chair rather than from his feet, while the port passed around. But it was a speech for all that, and it was equally as helpful to the Whigs as Colonel Dorking's. Telford was a worldly, interesting man, and he spoke with authority as to the influence of the bridge he was building and the advantage it would be to the town. Even Bathurst became interested, and Alistair was the keenest listener in the room, interrupting the speech occasionally with a pertinent question, usually having to do with some technical matter.

Reising could find no opening to mention the toll and was in a poor humor with his protégé, who actually sat praising the project! It was Hudson's turn to give a sympathetic smile to his rival. Tony was behaving pretty well, only mentioning a little more often than was necessary that it was to be known as the Fellows Bridge. But there was a definite wind of approval for Fellows in the air, and no one took exception to his repeated remarks.

After the port was finished, Dorking was taken to the parents of veterans and introduced to them. Then he spent some moments with the fathers of the two dead soldiers, and was invited in both cases to visit their homes on the morrow to meet the mothers. Both were Tory corn-growers, and Hudson was elated, but too clever to push either himself or Tony forward for the visit. This was not the time to push politics; he'd let Dorking, a confirmed Whig, do it for him.

The campaign was reaching its final phase. There was now less than a week to go till voting, and spirits were high in the Whig camp. Turning the riding seemed now not only possible but assured. Between the Fellows Bridge, the visit of Dorking to the veterans' do, and the subsequent pledge of a couple of farmers' votes during the house visits and the alienation of a few more from Tory ranks by the depredation on their pockets of the dashers from the city who had made known their preference for Mr. Alistair, it was beginning to look as though Mr. Fellows would get his Honorable and his M.P. He felt that his own dispensing of the *sine qua non*'s had also been instrumental, though Mr. Alistair had come down more heavily in that department recently, and in fact Hudson found his candidate a particularly clutch-fisted man.

The gentlemen had not lately been to New Moon, but after Dorking left and they had nothing more pressing to do than go and admire the bridge site and go into the stores for a chat and a small purchase or two, they took time one morning to drop in on the ladies, their first supporters. Fellows had to repeat to them a jumbled version of a bon mot of Telford's having to do with the bridge leading not only to Chepstow, across the river, but to London as well—for Mr. Fellows. He hadn't quite understood the joke, but everyone had laughed, so he knew it was clever.

"By Jove, it's a capital bridge," he began. "It not only goes north to Chepstow, but is to be turned around and take me south, eh Matt?"

The ladies naturally looked confused. "That's right. The bridge is to carry the Honorable Anthony Fellows to Parliament," Matt explained.

"You want to be careful, Mr. Fellows," Sara adjured him. "I wouldn't go on it for the world, and if they are to be moving it about, it will be even more unstable."

"It's a little joke, you see, Miss Monteith," Fellows explained to her. Certainly everyone had laughed last night at the Cat's Paw when Telford had said it. "They ain't really going to move the bridge, I believe. No such thing, eh, Matt?"

"That's right? It's just a joke."

"Weighs a ton," Fellows went on. "The way of it is, I won't go on the bridge at all. I'll take the road and my carriage to London. My traveling carriage—and I think I should take my curricle too, don't you, Matt?"

"Yes, certainly. You won't want to lumber around the city in a traveling carriage."

"Well then, it's not a bridge to London," Sara pointed out. She had been perusing her papa's map lately to see how far away Mr. Alistair would be when he went to London, and had discovered that London was on the same side of the river as Crockett. Not very far away, either— only about an inch, which couldn't be very far, even in miles.

"Dash it, you don't need a bridge to get to London. There's a road goes straight south. The river is to the north," Fellows said, becoming angry.

"London is to the east, is it not?" Martha asked.

"South to Bath, I mean, then east," Fellows said knowingly.

"That's what I said," Sara told him. "You don't need the bridge to go to London."

"Ho ho, I see your point now, clever minx. She's right, Matt. The bridge don't lead to London in the least. It's the member from the north of us will take the bridge to London."

"Very true. I think you'd better just forget Telford's little joke about the bridge leading to London," Hudson agreed, seeing what a quagmire his candidate would fall into every time he tried to repeat it.

"And him in charge of building roads." Anthony shook his head. "It's a caution how fellows end up with jobs they aint suited for in the least."

"Some Fellows certainly do," Lillian said, risking a covert glance at Mr. Hudson.

"It's a wonder they let him do it, and he not knowing south from north," Fellows said. "But he's got the right spot for my bridge all right and tight. I saw the pilings going in, and they're right where the bridge is to go."

"That's lucky," Sara said.

"Shall we all run down and have a look at it?" Fellows asked, not having been there for over twelve hours. He enjoyed very much the sign announcing the new Fellows Bridge, and would enjoy it even more the day he could add the magic letters M.P. to the sign.

"I've had about enough of the bridge," Hudson remarked. "We were going to visit that family to the west today, Tony; Armstrong I think is the name. We haven't been to see them at all."

"Waste of time," Tony informed him. "Old Armstrong

is on his deathbed. We'll not get him hauled to the polls. He'll never get to see the Fellows Bridge, poor soul."

"Still, I think I'll ride over and pay Armstrong a call. It's a pleasant day for a drive. I'll take my curricle. Perhaps one of you would like to come with me?" His question was flung in the general direction of Miss Watters, but Mr. Hudson was not only nearly invisible but also inaudible to her since so often aiding Miss Ratchett up the ravine. She pointedly paid no attention him.

"Miss Watters, would you care to come with me?" he was forced to ask directly.

"Sara might like to go," she replied.

"Nossir, I'm taking Miss Sara to see my bridge," Fellows jumped in, determined not to get stuck with that stiff-faced Miss Watters, as he saw developing.

"I don't want to go to the bridge," Sara objected.

"She wouldn't like that, Tony," Hudson said blandly. "There will be Alistair and a bunch hanging around, you know, as they always are."

"That's true." Tony relented, not liking to pitch Miss Sara into such company.

"Oh, maybe I *would* like to go," Sara said, considering the matter further.

"We'll cross that bridge when we come to it, eh?" Fellows said to her, meaning heaven only knew what.

"I must warn you, Alistair is always there," Hudson repeated, to secure her going.

"In that case, I'll get my pelisse," she said, and ran off.

"Miss Watters, will you come with me?" Hudson repeated.

"I'm getting a headache," she answered.

"The fresh air will do you good," Martha intervened,

seeing that it was Lillian Hudson preferred today. Really, the man was as fickle as Fate.

"Yes, you girls run along and get some exercise," Lady Monteith added, and got her own exercise by reaching for a bonbon.

"Very well," Lillian said, not averse to going so long as it was clear to Mr. Hudson that she was going against her will.

The two carriages set off, and very pleased Martha was to see both nieces sitting beside gentlemen of means for an unexceptionable outing.

"I think we have managed this pretty well," she remarked to Melanie.

"I told you it would be no job at all to get Sara a match."

"She hasn't got him yet, and what you must do, Melanie, is invite both of them to remain to lunch when they come back."

"We'll do that," Melanie agreed easily. She was not at all against socializing, so long as it did not involve much exertion to herself.

While Sara and Fellows went to look at the pilings for the bridge, and at the sign, and also at Mr. Alistair, who was there as promised and very attentive to Sara, Hudson and Lillian drove off to the west to visit the last uncanvassed voter.

"Have you really got a headache?" he asked her.

"I wouldn't say so if I didn't," she answered shortly.

"Did you have it before I arrived, or did I bring it with me?"

"I have had it all morning."

"I'll tell you what we'll do. After we have been to see Armstrong, I'll drop you off at the eye doctor, for I think it is your eyes that are causing your headache. They are failing on you, my girl. Twice this week I have nodded and waved to you, and you didn't appear to see me either time."

"There's nothing wrong with my eyes. They see more than you might think."

"They don't see quite *what* you think, however. I must be polite with Miss Ratchett when her father is so heavily into this bridge with me. I thought you understood that."

"Miss Ratchett has nothing to do with my headache, I assure you, and it is presumptuous of you to think so."

"We can't control our thoughts, presumptuous devils that they are. But I should have controlled my speech if you truly have a headache and didn't wish to come. I thought it was merely a fit of pique. I'll take you home if you like."

"Suit yourself," she replied with great indifference, while raging inside at the suggestion.

"I am trying to suit you, and mighty hard you're making it for me, Miss Watters. Home or not?"

"You have already gone half a mile. There's no point turning back now."

"We haven't gone ten yards. If you mean to sit and sulk the whole trip, I might as well be alone."

"I didn't realize it was my chore to beguile the hours for you while you drive, but I might have known you had some job for me to do!"

This encouraging reply prevented his turning the carriage around, as he was feeling strongly inclined to do. "Is it a fight you want? I'm not in the mood to comply today; I am too happy after the veterans' dinner. A great success, you know. Perhaps you heard?"

She had, but not from him, and there was the offense.

The several days of neglect had frayed her nerves and sharpened her temper. "I heard Colonel Dorking came and drummed up a few votes for you with his wooden leg. There is no cheap trick you wouldn't sink to to get a vote—making hay out of a wounded veteran!"

"You can't make bricks without straw. I am coming to rival Tony with my rapid epigrams, don't you think?" He smiled, but there was no response from his wooden-faced companion, so he changed his tack. "The Tories are treating the vets badly, and it is a fair thing to point it out, in my view."

"Fair! Much you care whether it's fair or not. You'd have your own mother out stumping for you if you thought it would do any good."

"She stumped for me regularly in Kent, but I didn't drag her around the countryside to every by-election. She was always my hostess, but she is dead now, unfortunately."

"You think to make me feel guilty by mentioning that, I suppose? I shouldn't be surprised if it was your shenanigans that killed her."

"You're wrong—she delighted in them. I couldn't keep her nose out of my business. There was nothing she liked so much as a good, dirty fight. She taught me half of what I know. I thought you enjoyed it too. It was your suggestion, if you will recall, that we supply Tony with prearranged questions, and you gave me the idea of bringing in Dorking. Now you throw it in my face."

"I never heard of the man till *you* spoke of him."

"It was Wellington you actually mentioned, but that was impossible. Bringing a soldier-hero here was your idea, and don't trouble to deny it. It was an excellent idea, too—worthy of my mother. A conniving female's brain is a great help in work of this sort. They outdistance us simple men every time. Do you not think you would enjoy being involved in the world of politics?"

There were overtones to the question that were not to be ignored. How should she be involved in such a world but through him, and how should any involvement with him be kept up after this by-election except through marrying him? "I think it is a good deal too rackety for me," she said, and waited to be dissuaded.

"You don't know yourself. You would love it. Oh, it comes as a little surprise the first time you realize there is some bribery involved, but you realize that now, and the next time you wouldn't give it a thought. Your only interest would be how much, and could you afford it, and if not, what trick could you turn to come up with the money."

"Very tempting, that I should become so gross I no longer recognized wrongdoing for wrongdoing! It is a sordid business, and I don't know why you choose to involve yourself in it when you don't have to."

"Someone has to. If we leave it to the real crooks, only think what a state the country would be in. I have nothing to gain by it. I'm not after the money—I have that. And I'm not power-hungry or I would have got myself elected a Tory before this. I genuinely believe my party is not so bad as the other. There are some bad men in it, self-seeking men, as there are in any party or church or any other institution. Politics turns a good many honest men off by its reputation, but if the honest men refuse to fight for what they believe is right, what chance has the country? And once you are in a fight, you know, there's no point pussyfooting around in velvet gloves when your opponent is wielding an ax. You're either in a fight to win or you stay out. I'm in. For life, I think. When I inherit from my uncle I will be a member of Lords—a much more dignified gentleman altogether, and no longer out ripping barn doors off their hinges—but it is only the details that will change. I'll still be fighting, using every dirty trick I know to gain a point. You find that unacceptably sordid?"

"It's nothing to me how you choose to spend your life," she answered, waiting with bated breath for a clearer statement of how it should become something to her.

"I'm asking you for an opinion, Miss Watters. Do you find such a life disgusting?"

"Everyone to his taste."

"What about *your* taste?"

"I never gave it much thought. I don't foresee that I am likely to be engaged in anything of the sort myself. That is for men to worry about."

"And men's families, surely?" If only he had used the word "wives" he might have saved himself a great deal of time, but the vague "families" allowed her to misunderstand.

"Your mother had no objections, in any case."

He signed wearily. "Whatever you think, we'll never know. You are a born politician, so cautious one would think you were already in office. I never heard one yet would admit he was standing where he was, or that it was Monday, or October, or anything else that was perfectly clear to everyone. They must always leave the door open to change their minds and throw in a dozen 'in certain cases' and 'under given circumstances' and the like. I hope to God I don't turn into that sort of a mealy-mouthed fellow, who doesn't stand for anything."

"You've made it pretty clear what you stand for. You

stand for getting that clothhead of a Fellows into Parliament, and you will use whatever expedient you must to achieve it. You know perfectly well Alistair is worth ten of him, and you should be ashamed to hold up your head after the way you have carried on." All this was the result of his implying she was mealy-mouthed, and his reply to it was largely founded on her praise of Alistair.

"You would be hard put to prove I have harmed anyone. Several of the merchants are better off than they were before."

"All of them! You didn't miss anyone with your bribery, did you?"

"I hope not. Crockett is getting a bridge at last."

"One they will have to pay for every time they want to use it."

"And don't forget to tell everyone how frightfully unsafe it is! Who are you taking lessons from, Sara or Alistair?"

"Mr. Alistair, for I find him better informed on all matters than either Sara or Fellows."

"Or Hudson. What has Mr. Alistair to say about Corporal Winton being given the job of collecting tolls on the bridge? What smear has he worked into that?"

"You will do admirably in Parliament, Mr. Hudson. You whitewash all your black tricks and make a piddling little sinecure seem a matter of importance."

"Your tongue outruns me; I can't get the answer to a simple, straightforward question from you. Do you hate what I am doing? Do you dislike it so much you would object to being part of it?" He looked at her expectantly and somewhat angrily.

"It's nothing to me how you spend your time and

money," she answered, but her heart raced and her head was light with the significance of the question.

He stared at her a moment, then let out a chuckle. "That will teach me to try to make up to a girl with a headache. Think about what I asked you after your migraine has passed away. As soon as you manage to escape me, in other words. That is two things I have given you to think about. You never did come up with a bribe for me to tell you about the bridge, and I told you anyway, but that doesn't mean I'll let you off the hook this time. You must make up your own mind about this, Lillian. It would be dishonest of me to tell you I will change, for I don't think I could. I don't ask you to change either, if you truly dislike what I am doing. I wish you would try to like it, however," he finished up, and her headache was forgotten.

# 12

THE Armstrong farm was five miles down the road, and by turning the conversation to the scenery and other innocuous subjects, they completed the trip without another word of interest being said. Mr. Armstrong inhabited a large, square brick home, solid without being in any way luxurious. His wife answered her own door and admitted the callers. She had three young girls in the house with her, daughters who were at an age where they would have been in the schoolroom still had their help not been necessary around the house. Lillian took the mother for a woman in her forties, for her eye was bright in spite of the haggard expression she wore.

She and Hudson sat for a quarter of an hour talking to Mrs. Armstrong without the subject of politics arising at all. By a series of discreet questions it came out that she was perfectly aware her husband was dying, and having come to terms with this, she was quite properly directing her thoughts to keeping her family together. Her eldest son, Isaac, would have to take over the farm, and he was a bookish sort of a lad, not well-equipped for the job. She had a bachelor brother who would be happy to help her, but of course such a man would be an additional expense to the family.

After all this was talked over, Hudson was taken up to see Mr. Armstrong. He descended after ten minutes looking grave, and she didn't bother with the farce of mentioning a recovery. The back-slapping, joking politician was not in evidence today. Mrs. Armstrong showed them to the door. "Isaac will be in Crockett tomorrow, ma'am?" Hudson queried just before leaving.

"Yes, he goes every second day to help out at the newspaper office. He's only twenty-two, but very clever. He does a bit of writing up for them. Very excited he is about the bridge, Mr. Hudson. He says it will be a fine thing for the town."

This was as close to politicking as they came. "He's right. Will you tell him I'll drop in at the office and see him then?"

"He'll be pleased to meet you," she said, smiling on top of her cares. It was a pitiful sight.

A strained silence sat in the curricle with its occupants on the way back to New Moon. "Mr. Armstrong is too ill to get out and vote, I presume?" Lillian asked, as that was the only reason she knew of for the call.

Hudson looked surprised at her question. "He'll be dead before the week's out," he answered with conviction.

"Poor woman, and she with three young girls to raise, two of them with their hair not up yet. How will she manage?"

"She'll manage if she has to work her fingers to the bone to do it. That was a lady you just met, Lillian. Don't let the cotton gown and the apron fool you. I take my hat off to her. It does a ruined soul like myself good to bump into a person like that once in a while. She asks nothing from life but half a chance to take care of herself and her family. If this Isaac is as clever as she thinks, they'll manage. It makes you wonder, doesn't it, why such a catastrophe should befall them, while the Sinclairs and Fellows and Hudsons of the world go merrily on their way without a hitch?"

The trip home was not lively, but it was not argumentative, at least, and when they reached New Moon, Hudson accepted an invitation to lunch. Tony was there; he and Sara had returned more than an hour ago, but it did not occur to him, apparently, to go out and do anything on his own hook, for which all concerned had reason to be grateful. He was holding Sara's wools while she wound them into balls, under the Argus eyes of Martha. Hudson outlined the morning he and Lillian had spent.

"Told you it was a waste of time," Tony reproached

him. "Armstrong will never make it to the polls. At least it won't be a vote for the Tories."

Hudson ignored this solecism and began to discuss the heavy load of work Tony would be saddled with once he was elected. His election was now spoken of as quite a certain thing. "And when you're in London, you will want someone here in your riding to keep an eye on things. Someone to keep you informed."

Tony glanced at Sara, of all unlikely people. "Mr. Alistair is always well-informed on everything," she suggested.

"I meant someone in your employ, to handle your correspondence for you," Hudson enlarged.

"Peagoose!" Martha muttered in the direction of her younger niece, but after an hour in the company of this pair of wise ones, she was not surprised.

"A secretary is what I need," Tony decided, elated to be a man of so much consequence.

"Yes, that's what I meant. Some sharp young fellow to act as a right-hand man for you."

"How about that Corporal Winton—oh, but he's got no right arm. I don't want a left-hand man. Pity I couldn't give it to a decapitated veteran."

"It would be preferable, I think, if he had his head about him," Hudson said grimly.

"Oh, if it's head you want, Basingstoke is our man. As longheaded as may be," Tony said.

"He lives too far away, and Corporal Winton is to be the toll collector on the Fellows Bridge."

"So he is. I forgot we'd managed to find a job for the poor soul that he can handle with his one wing."

"We were fortunate enough to get Winton to take the

post," Hudson corrected, without much hope that the words would be remembered.

"*We* were fortunate! Why, everyone and his mother has been pestering me for the post. He's the lucky one to get any sort of a job—mutilated and unable to do a real day's work. It's the Whigs that did it for him, eh, Matt?"

"That's right, Tony. About a secretary for you . . . I hear the young Armstrong fellow is bright. Does a bit of writing for the local paper."

"Writes such stuff as Miss Jones is gone to Bath to visit her aunt, and Mrs. Purdy is in bed with the gout. He ain't a real writer."

"He wrote a pretty fine piece about the Fellows Bridge last week. I mean to ask the paper to send it to London for printing in the *Gazette*."

"Dash it, Tony, you said everything we give away must bring in a vote. We don't have to get him a job; his father ain't voting at all."

"His father isn't voting because he is dying, and the family is in great difficulty. But that is nothing to the point," he added quickly, to prevent the offer being put to Armstrong in this light. "He is a local chap, young and alert. If he will take the job, he is the very one to help you. His working for the local paper is a good circumstance too. I'd let him keep that up as well; he only works there every second day. He would be the perfect answer to your problem."

"I'll think it over," Fellows stated importantly.

"You should interview him. He'll be at the newspaper office tomorrow," Hudson mentioned.

Conducting an interview sounded a pleasant and consequential pastime, and Fellows agreed to it with no difficulty. When the two of them were alone, Hudson continued to pound into his head the need for a secretary and the advantage of having a secretary in a position to insert complimentary pieces in the local paper. By the time the call was paid, Fellows was eager to engage Mr. Armstrong and didn't say much in the way of unwitting insult, except that he was glad to be able to give him a hand, even if he wasn't a veteran, and how did it come he'd shied away from the war anyway—he a strapping young man of one hundred and ten pounds, wearing thick glasses.

It was the very day after they hired Isaac Armstrong that his father died, but this fact was overborne by a much worse one for the Whigs. Hudson's first inkling of it occurred in the village. He was with Mr. Fellows, again visiting the open market stalls, when Reising and Alistair were seen across the way, in more cheerful humor than they had been in since the coming to Crockett of the bridge and Colonel Dorking.

"What have that pair got to grin about?" Hudson asked uneasily.

"They are putting a good face on their defeat," Tony told him, this having been drummed into his head as a necessary thing when it seemed he would be the defeated candidate. It seemed the likely reason, for the cheering mob that used to trail at Alistair's heels was now at Tony's. He was already being treated as the member for the riding, with citizens beginning to come to him with their problems for advice and help.

Hudson had been through many campaigns with Reising, and he thought the gloating face of his old rival denoted more than acquiescence to defeat. Reising was a notably poor loser. Hudson had been waiting for reprisals ever since the coming of Telford, had even been a little uneasy at the lack of them, for he knew Reising was a sly old fox who would stick at nothing. He began to edge his way toward the Tory pair, a thing Reising would normally have welcomed, as it brought the mob into a position where they might be taken to be huddling around Alistair. But on this occasion Reising kept moving away.

"There's something amiss," Hudson fretted. "Tony, did anything happen yesterday when you took Sara down to the bridge?"

"Yes, by Jove. Alistair was there making up to Sara something awful." This had been a bit of a problem from the beginning, for the attraction between them was no secret to anyone. But still Hudson could not see why this should set Reising to gloating, and if anything notable had happened, he believed he would have heard of it before now.

"What exactly went on?"

"They was both putting down my bridge, Sara saying it wasn't safe and Alistair griping about the tolls, and he as rich as a nabob. He can walk across if he don't want to pay the toll, and I won't charge him a penny, and so I told him too."

Neither of these complaints was new or likely to be the cause of the glee in the enemy camp, for it was becoming clearer by the minute that Reising was in alt about something.

"What did you say to them?"

"Just what you told me, Matt. Said it was safe as a church, and had never killed a soul or fallen or a thing in America. I said the tolls was only for carriages, and I'd let the poor go on foot for free."

"That's good, Tony. Remember those two points. Was there anything else?"

"Well, it came out that that sneak of a Sara was giving out pamphlets for Alistair, but that was early on, the day she and her mama went around to the shops for us to send all them wilted turnips and what-not to the orphanage and poorhouse."

"Was she, by God! And none of them mentioning a word of it to us. She must have known."

"Course she knew! She had them hid in her reticule. I've been telling you all along she's a clever puss."

"I meant Miss Watters, but it can't be that they're smirking about. That was weeks ago. You should have told me though. Always tell me everything, Tony. You haven't gone and pitched yourself into a duel or anything of that sort, have you?"

"What, with Alistair? I ain't such a flat as that. He's a devil with his pops. Could hit a bull's-eye across a field. Nossir, I don't hold with dueling."

"You have no idea what's going on then?"

"They're putting a good face on their defeat. It's the only course open to them now that they've lost."

Matt found it impossible to be certain yet that they had lost, and when Reising and Alistair turned to leave the market, he was after them, risking leaving Fellows alone with his admirers for five minutes. Reising turned to see Hudson and waited for him. "How's your lover-boy to-day?" he asked in a tone of heavy sarcasm.

Matthew breathed a sigh of relief, thinking it was only some nonsense to do with Sara. "In high gig, as you must have seen for yourself just now."

"He won't be in such high gig when it gets out what he's been up to."

"People take a lenient view of bachelors' making up to

the ladies. Alistair has been doing a spot of wooing of his own, I hear."

"Ha ha—but Mr. Alistair is more discreet. He restricts himself to single ladies, and to the spoken word, too. You might warn your man of the danger of *billets doux* to married ladies. I'm surprised you haven't done so."

Admitting ignorance was something never done by either whipper-in, and Hudson swallowed the lump in his throat, preparatory to trying to discover what that ass of a Tony had been up to behind his back.

"You have managed to get a copy of the letter, I assume?" he asked, hoping to get a look at what was being spoken of, to see just how damning it was and of course to whom it was addressed.

"No, Hudson, I have the originals." Reising smiled and pulled out three pieces of paper. Hudson recognized Tony's round writing at a glance. He reached out a hand for them, but Reising drew them back.

"You'll have to wait and read them in a special pamphlet we are having prepared," he said. "We mean to distribute it the day before the election—tomorrow, that is. I expect young Miss Monteith will help us circulate them." A gratuitous blow, but hardly important. It was imperative to see just how damaging the letters were.

"May I have a look?" Hudson asked, showing no more than mild curiosity.

"Let him, Reising," Alistair said, laughing. "Mr. Hudson may decide to withdraw his candidate and save us the expense, and Lady Marie the embarrassment, of distributing them."

Lady Marie! Good God, that fat yellow-haired Tory wife of Sir John Sinclair! But it was Basingstoke who was spoken of as her hopeful lover. Hudson, with the cool nerve of an assassin, reached out an unshaking hand for the letters. He read through them quickly, pretending to do no more than glance at them, but many phrases were indelibly printed on his mind. It was drivel of the worst sort, extremely damning drivel, couched in ardent schoolboy's prose. He wondered how Reising had got hold of them and that Lady Marie should let them out of her own hands for a minute.

"Sir John won't appreciate having this bruited about," he said, this being the only possible response he could think of on the spur of the moment. "A backhanded trick to serve your heaviest supporter. I have heard a thousand pounds mentioned as his contribution." Hudson knew it was seven hundred and fifty pounds to a penny Sir John had kicked in, but the managers always feigned a little more ignorance than they possessed as a basic tactic.

"Oh, he's a good sport. He don't take it amiss that his wife is a handsome woman. No secret Basingstoke takes to her, and while it won't add to her reputation to have attached such a gudgeon as Fellows, it is pretty clear from the tone of the letters that there was no reciprocation of feeling. The last one, you will notice, is all to do with her not bestowing so much as a glance or a smile on him. It appears to have been a one-sided affair, which says a good deal for the lady's common sense."

"Publishing them says little for her discretion."

"A case of the pot calling the kettle black, Mr. Hudson. Your allowing Fellows to go calling on his amour in the middle of a campaign is a piece of indiscretion on your part that quite baffles me. I don't know what you thought to gain by it, but whatever it was, it backfired. It was the very thing that made Sir John suspicious and then angry enough to allow the letters to be published."

Hudson would as soon have cut off his arm as admit he had bungled, so he only smiled as if he were concealing some devious trick.

"In a small community like ours, carrying-on of this sort will be taken very ill," Alistair pointed out. "Well, what do you say, Mr. Hudson? Do you wish to withdraw Fellows?"

Hudson had been considering this in the half-minute allowed him for planning, but was not ready to capitulate so easily. By pretending to, though, he might delay publication till it was too late to circulate the letters. "Let me think about it," he said carelessly.

"Go ahead. You have till tomorrow," Alistair told him.

"Meanwhile we've had the copies printed up," Reising added, "in case you're thinking to stall us off."

It flashed into Hudson's head that he must break into the newspaper printing office and purloin the letters, and the next moment he was juggling Isaac Armstrong against his own flash culls for the job. The city crooks had been kept in town in case of just such an emergency as this. But Reising was no Johnnie Raw, and knew precisely what was in his mind.

"They're not being done in Crockett, of course," Reising informed him with a grin. "The story would be around by now if we'd done that, and we hope to keep it for a bit of a surprise. They'll be on the streets tomorrow morning."

"Had them printed in London, did you?" Hudson asked nonchalantly.

"No, I didn't, Hudson, and there's no point trying to find out where they were printed, for I don't have a mind to have them snatched by your fellows before they get on the streets. We may have them all printed up and secured, or we may have them coming to us from any direction, and not even you, old friend, can canvass so many possibilities in less than twenty-four hours. You've got yourself saddled with a rare boy this time. You nearly pulled it off—I take my hat off to you about the bridge and the dinner—but not even you could have foreseen this turn. You know where you can reach us if you decide to pull Fellows out. We ain't anxious to drag Lady Marie into it, but we have her permission, and Sir John is eager to see the riding in Tory hands, so there's no hope they'll go denying the authenticity of the letters."

"I didn't think you'd stoop to blackmail, Reising," Hudson said in a severe tone.

Alistair, really still a novice at this game, felt cheap to be looked down on by Mr. Hudson, who seemed every inch the fine gentleman, with his gray-tinged hair, his pending title, and his noble countenance.

"Ha ha, not much you didn't!" Reising laughed merrily, having a much more accurate knowledge of his opponent. "You'd have done the same thing yourself if you'd had the chance or the necessity. I don't suppose you forget the night you barged into the George at Reading to catch MacIntosh, my boy, with that young trollop he'd picked up in the tavern. And it was you set her on to him too, if I know anything—and then brought half the voters in the county with you to catch him."

"I didn't set her on to him. That is one trick of yours I refuse to use. But when a clergyman runs on the strength of his moral principles, it is only fair that his constituents know how closely he follows his own advice."

"I didn't blame you. It was a cute trick, but I've got

you this time. I owe you one for MacIntosh, and by God it gives me pleasure to repay you."

"You haven't repaid me yet, Reising. I'll be in touch," Hudson said, and left with a wry smile that turned to a desperate grimace as he turned his back on them and went to the market to collect Tony.

He found him in the middle of a crowd, expounding his views on the Tories. "Blackguards, every one of them. I wouldn't trust them with a penny, or with my sister either, if I had one."

Hudson groaned at the irony of it and managed to get his candidate away by implying there was weighty business to discuss. As soon as they were in their carriage, away from the crowd, Hudson put it to him.

"You wrote love-letters to Lady Marie Sinclair?" he asked, though he had no doubts at all regarding those disastrous scribbles.

Fellows blushed and looked a little sheepish. "Lord, how did you tumble to that? It was six months ago. Me and Basingstoke was both after her, but she seemed to favor Basingstoke's suit. Of course he was living closer to her and could go in person to butter her up. I had to rely on letters, and nothing came of it. Writing letters ain't my strong suit, to tell the truth."

"You never actually had an affair with her?"

"No, no, and don't believe I would have had she given in either, for she's a bit long in the tooth to suit my taste. Basingstoke thought she was all the crack, and he's so longheaded, you know, that if he likes her, she must be a bit of all right."

"Oh God, you're hopeless."

"No, no, there was never a thing to it, I swear. I mind

Allingham asked me before they put me up to run if there was anything in my past that would disgrace me if it came out, and he mentioned a mistress in particular, and my hands are clean."

"The hands have nothing to do with it. Those letters are as incriminating as hell. You asked her to be your mistress."

"Well, dash it, you've got to say something in a love-letter! I didn't mean it. I'd have palmed her off on Basingstoke if it had ever come down to it," Fellows said defensively.

"Reising has the letters and means to publish them. We're finished; you're disgraced. You should have told me—I've asked you a dozen times to tell me anything that might be of interest."

"I didn't know you was interested in my letters or I'd have told you, Matt. Truth to tell, I thought she'd got rid of them. She said she would, as I destroyed hers."

"You had replies to them! When was this? What was in them?"

"Why, the softest muck you ever heard of. Calling me a naughty boy and saying as how she looked forward to seeing me at some party or other and all sorts of things. She was half-gone on me, if you want the truth. I never let on to Basingstoke, but I think I might have had her for the taking if I'd kept after it. But I eased off somewhat, you know, and then she cooled down. I only wrote once after that, for I felt I was pretty safe; I jawed her out a bit for being cool to me, but the fact of the matter is I was relieved."

"And you destroyed her letters! You got rid of that good evidence! Tony—oh, what's the use! Does she know they're destroyed?" he asked, hoping yet for a reprieve

by a little blackmail of his own if he could lead Reising
to believe he had the answers.

"Yes, I got rid of them, Matt, so you needn't fear
they'll publish her answers. And she knows it, for I did it
right in front of her eyes."

"Marvelous!"

"Yessir, they can't go stealing her answers and publishing them. She asked me to get rid of them, and truth to
tell I wasn't half-eager to have them sitting around the
house where the servants might stumble on them, for
they root around when you ain't home, no denying."

"Why didn't you get yours back?"

"She said she'd get rid of them. It was at a do at my
place she asked me for hers, and I tossed 'em right into
the fire before her very eyes, and she said she'd do the
same with mine the minute she got home, so how is it
possible you've seen them?"

"She gave them to Reising. He's going to publish them
for the whole town to snicker over and see what a damned
fool you are!"

"She couldn't bear to part with them when it came
down to it. And you know how the girls like to brag
about having landed a fellow. As to using them, well,
they're all Tories together. They haven't seen the light.
You can't really blame them. Basingstock wouldn't have
been sweet on Marie if she ain't the goods, so there's
nothing to be ashamed of in it. Anyway, nobody will believe a word of it. They'll think it's just a low Tory trick,
for I've been telling them this very morning that you can't
trust a Tory."

"You can trust a Tory to publish those letters, believe
me. What are we to do?"

"It's just as you said. They're using one of them cheap *hominem* things, abusing me, and so I'll tell the world."

"You've got to withdraw. It's the only thing. You won't get a single vote."

"I'll get Basingstoke's and Allingham's, for Basingstoke knows all about my letters and he didn't take it amiss in the least since I backed off. And I'll get *my* vote."

"Three votes won't carry you to London."

"There's the bridge. And how about all them *sine qua non*'s we've been spending in the village? Wearing this ugly old lid of Saunders's too."

"That bastard of a Reising has outwitted me. I don't know where he's got the printed pamphlets and I haven't time to find them. You have to pull out. You can claim ill health. A soft brain would be credible, I think."

"What, pull out and hand it to Alistair on a platter! Where's your wits, Hudson? This is a man's game. If we can't take a little *ad hominem* we ain't the sort to be in politics in the first place. Far as that goes, I ain't ashamed of making up to Marie. You'd be surprised at the chicks dangling after me since I'm into politics. That Miss Ratchett has been telling me a dozen times how she'd love to live in London, and she means with me, make no mistake about that. You ain't the only one she's been casting her line at, so don't think it. Her old man's rolling in money too. Why, I daresay they'll all take me for a great fellow, having such a knowing flirt as Lady Marie. Only fancy her wanting to get my letters copied to go bragging to her friends. I daresay she thought no one would believe her if she didn't show 'em the letters."

Hudson had his ears half turned off, and only looked his reproach.

"In the usual way I don't bother much about the girls,

you know," Fellows rattled on. "They're trying to foist young Miss Monteith on me, as you may have noticed. The chicks will all be jealous as green cows."

"It's not the chicks will be voting. It's their fathers and husbands, and if you think any husband relishes the thought of your dangling after his wife behind his back, you're a maw-worm."

"Lord, they will be taking me for a wild buck," Fellows chuckled, very well pleased with this novel turn to his dull reputation.

"I'm pulling you out of the race. You have to know when you're finished."

"No, by God, I ain't pulling out. I've laid down a load of blunt to be an Honorable M.P.—five hundred pounds of it. I've worn this old hat for weeks, I've as good as promised I'd show Miss Ratchett the town when she comes to London, and I've made dozens of promises to my constitutents. I can't let them down."

"Tony, you're not going to be the Honorable Member for the riding. You're going to be the laughingstock of the town if you let Reising print those letters. You've lost, and as you are going to be staying here as plain Mr. Fellows, you might as least stop the circulation of the pamphlet and save any shred of dignity you can."

"Ho, dignity! What has that to say to anything? The Prince of Wales himself is pelted with mud when he goes about in London. And he has a mistress too. I ain't ashamed of doing what the Prince of Wales does. No harm in it. Besides, I never had a thing to do with Lady Marie but write her a few love-letters. If Alistair puts it about that I actually am her lover, I'll—well, I'll let the town know what a low Tory he is."

"You're withdrawing. I withdraw the party's support

from you, and if you insist on running, you must do so as
an Independent. I won't have the party smeared with this
sort of muck. There is nothing to be gained by it." This
was, of course, only an empty threat. Fellows was so
closely allied with the Whig label that even if he could
withdraw party support—which he couldn't do with only
one day to get in touch with London—the blame would
be attached to the party.

"I'll run as an Independent then," Fellows replied without a moment's hesitation. "They'll all be after me when
I get to the House, both Whigs and Tories."

Now how the devil did the dolt twig to that? On the one
chance in a million that he might still win his seat, Hudson
was forced to conciliate him. He was clearly determined to
make a fool of himself and it appeared to be beyond
Hudson's power to prevent it. He took Fellows home and
warned him that to save his life he must not leave the
abbey, or see anyone there.

"I'll do just as you say, Matt, and I know we'll get in.
I don't despair, for you're a very good manager. Basingstoke told me so."

Even in the midst of his anger with Tony, Hudson felt
a twinge of compassion for him. He wanted this job so
very much and had spent such a lot of money to get it
that it seemed a shame a fat old lady should be able to
snatch it from his hands. And he might not be such a bad
member either, for he was so eager for everyone's adula-
tion that he would work like a dog to get what they
wanted.

Hudson drove his curricle to New Moon. He wanted
to discuss it with Lillian. He was by no means sure of
sympathy from her, but he wanted very much to be with
her.

*13*

❧❧❧❧❧❧❧❧❧❧❧❧❧❧❧❧❧❧❧❧❧❧❧❧❧❧❧❧❧❧

AFTER a careful consideration of her discussion with Mr. Hudson on the trip to the bridge site, Lillian could see nothing else in it than a forerunner to a proposal. She had bungled the matter badly and now was waiting impatiently for a chance to do better. When Mr. Hudson came to New Moon with the express purpose of asking her and no one else to ride out with him, her spirits soared. He was going to offer—she felt it could be no less than an offer—and her Aunt Martha was not less optimistic. She gave her gracious consent to both the drive and the marriage, the former orally, the latter in her heart, eyes, and every rapturous line of her body.

But Lillian knew as soon as they were alone that it was not marriage or any other happy matter to be discussed. She had never seen Mr. Hudson so blue. "What is the matter? Why are you so glum, Mr. Hudson? You ought to be happy. You have as well as got Mr. Fellows elected. Everyone says so."

"No, I haven't, Lillian," he said in a restrained voice.

"Has something happened today? At the market this morning everyone was crowding around him."

"Were you there? I didn't see you."

"We saw you," she said rather shyly. "But you left before you saw us. Has Fellows said something foolish? I wondered at your going after Reising and leaving him all alone."

"Oh, said! Words are written on air. You can always wiggle out of a spoken statement—pretend you were misunderstood or misquoted or meant something else entirely. He has committed his deathless words to paper this time. And what words!"

"What has he done to upset you so?"

At her sympathetic tone, he reached out and gripped her hand tightly. "He's sunk himself, the clunch. He has been writing love-letters to a local lady."

"Really! Can you beat that? I'd have thought him the last man in the world to be so dashing. But that is not so bad. He is a bachelor, after all. It will give him a touch of romance."

"A *married* lady!"

"Oh, dear. Who?"

"No need to name names. But a Tory, of course, to make it worse."

"You can't trust me, and I wearing my fingers to the bone for the cause?" she asked.

"Of course I trust you," he said with a smile, squeezing her fingers more tightly. "You are the only good thing that has happened to me in this campaign. But I wish you will not mention her name to the others, for there's a chance it will not come out. It's Lady Marie Sinclair— Sir John's wife. That awful-looking woman with the yellow curls and the shrill voice. And Basingstoke's flirt into the bargain."

"How incriminating are the letters?"

"Fatal—the worst drivel in the world, full of purple passages. Even an attempt at poetry. If she releases those letters, we're sunk."

"Surely she wouldn't. A married lady—she must look to her own reputation."

"What harm to her that Fellows makes a jackass of himself over her?"

"She didn't answer his letters at all?"

"Yes—some fine incriminating stuff, by all accounts— and he burned them. Can you beat his throwing away such useful evidence?"

"I can imagine his not holding on to love-letters with an eye to using them for blackmail, yes, but I expect it is pretty naive of me," she answered, but in no censorious way. She was careful to keep her tone light, teasing.

"Why will you always make me look a reptile? I know what you're going to say—why do I always act like one. But you see the sort of people I deal with. And the worst of it is, he never really had a thing to do with her, or even wanted to. It was Basingstoke's taking a shine to her that put the notion in his head. It stopped at the letters, but who will believe it?"

"It is a pity our candidate has no adultery to be boasted of!" she proclaimed.

"I didn't mean that! I meant—oh, you know perfectly well what I meant, and it is unkind of you to put the boots to me when I'm down. I don't know where you women get the reputation for being tenderhearted. Hearts of flint, those of you who have one at all."

"We wouldn't live long if we had no hearts."

"Oh, you have pumps in there, something to circulate the blood around. I'm talking about compassion. I doubt one woman in a hundred knows the meaning of the word. Now don't sulk, Lily. You know I adore squabbling with you, but what are we to do about these letters? The old bit - -, beast of a lady has given Reising carte blanche to publish them."

"Your intended epithet was not too harsh. My, how this will set her pride up, to be so singled out by him! He hardly looks at the ladies at all from what I can see. Even Sara, so lovely as she is, is hardly noticed. It is not only skinny sourpusses he holds in aversion. She will be greatly honored to be the only one noticed by him—quite a feather in her cap. A pity it is such a signal honor. When a man flirts with everyone, you know—not that *I* name names either—there is no special glory in having attached him; but this is something quite else."

"On behalf of all nameless curs everywhere I thank you for your reticence." He sat silent, thinking; then a slow, sneaky smile spread over his face. "But who says it was a signal honor? He has written such letters to dozens of girls."

"Has he indeed? Who else says so? Oh, there is no hope of keeping it silent in that case."

"No one else has said so, but they will, in droves."

"What do you mean?"

"I mean to increase the numbers of such epistles of his to such an absurd degree that she won't dare to breathe a word about hers. Every barmaid and milkmaid and lady's maid and lady of pleasure in the whole damned neighborhood will have had a similar letter from him—if only I can remember the words. If Lady Marie wishes to place herself on the level of her employees, and Leaky Peg at the Cat's Paw, and the acknowledged prostitutes in the town, I'll be greatly surprised."

"What are you talking about? He cannot have written so many."

"He will have—predated—and when I show Reising the batch of letters I've collected, Lady Marie will no more let him publish her own than she'll quit bleaching her hair."

"You can't do that! What a complete and utter fool he will look."

"He looks that anyway, so we have nothing to lose. It's a last, desperate gamble, but it might prevent them from publishing."

"You can't go using girls' names in that way. It's not fair."

"I'll butter 'em up with charm and the old *sine qua non*'s if they prove to be as hardhearted as yourself. What does Leaky Peg care if her name is linked with Tony's? She's not fussy. As far as that goes, I mean to do no more than wave the pile of letters under Reising's nose. Old Lady Bitch is running the show; if she tells him not to publish, he won't dare to do it. Anyway, what have we got to lose?"

"Mr. Hudson, you're a genius—an evil genius. I called you a Machiavelli, but that poor Italian innocent lamb wouldn't stand a chance against you."

"Fight fire with fire. It was you gave me the idea again, and I like it prodigiously. I've got to get busy and set Tony to penning up a batch of letters. I don't suppose you—no, the handwriting at least had better be authentic, since the date will not. Now how will I induce him to do it?"

She furrowed her brow in concentration. "Would it be possible to convince him of the truth?"

"No, he'd want to write his letters to you and Sara and Miss Ratchett, and the whole point of it is to make the crew as disreputable as possible. You are smiling—I suppose you like the idea of including Miss Ratchett well enough."

"Oh no, it is always you who wants to be including Miss Ratchett in everything."

"Not everything! I am formulating some plans from which she is excluded entirely, but I shouldn't be. I should be devising a way to get Tony to write these letters. Well, I'll tell him the gentry are wise enough to recognize his worth, but the ragtag and bobtail are so jealous that his only chance of getting elected is to write to their women. He's pretty humble at the moment, and if I get to him right away I may wheedle him into it. We're not done yet, Lil."

"*Lil?* This goes from bad to worse."

"Lillian, Lily—what name do you like?"

"My name is Miss Watters," she pointed out.

"No, I don't like that name at all. I think we should change it, don't you?" he asked with a smile.

"Not to Lil, if you please."

"That wasn't the change I had in mind. We'll fight it out later. Meanwhile, thank you once again for your help. Does this mean you have overcome your aversion to my sordid way of life, as you are again contributing to my little peccadilloes with your sage counsel?"

"*Little* peccadilloes!"

"You are quite right to point out the redundancy. A peccadillo is a little thing, a trifling sort of a fault."

"At least you acknowledge bribery and blackmail to be faults. I half-expected you would transform them into virtues."

"No, no, I acknowledge those little blemishes on my otherwise praiseworthy character. No one is perfect. And I still say you deserve credit for the idea."

"It wouldn't have occurred to me in a million years."

"You inspire me to evil genius and to all sorts of other evil thoughts. I had better take you home before you inspire me to action."

"Mr. Hudson, I wish you will behave."

"No, you don't," he laughed. "You've shown your true colors, milady. I won't have time to come by tonight. I have to visit the local ladies of pleasure, Leaky Peg et al. You can see I mean to pass a decorous evening, but it's all politics. And of course I shall get Tony to his desk and pay a call on Reising. How I look forward to that!"

"Will it work?" she asked with more eagerness than disapproval.

"Who knows? We can but try. Well, here we are home. Do you mind if I don't see you to the door? I have the

devil of a lot to do, and I don't think Aunt Martha is
peeking through the curtains. She would not have expected us back so soon."

"She doesn't peek through the curtains, and no one
gave you the right to call her Aunt Martha. I suppose I
must thank my stars I am not abandoned at the Cat's
Paw with Leaky Peg."

"No, really, I'm not that bad, am I?"

"You're worse!" she said, with such a beaming smile
that he left with no fear.


Tony proved so slow a penman that the list of recipients
was limited to Leaky Peg, two local prostitutes, and
Tony's own kitchen maid, but Reising was given to understand these were but a sample of the company in which
Lady Marie was to find herself if she had the letters published. The money to pay off the girls had to come out of
the party coffers, and Tony was told the story of rampant
jealousy in the village to get him to cooperate. He was
vastly flattered and wrote up such a load of tripe that
Matthew grabbed two spoiled letters to show Lillian,
knowing she wouldn't believe him without the proof.

After spending an extremely busy evening dashing
around from tavern to brothel to kitchen, Hudson paid
his highly anticipated call on Reising. He was prepared
for a regular set-to.

Alistair, who was visiting his whipper-in, was in high
glee to see Fellows an even worse fool than he had
hitherto suspected. "The man has ruined himself!" he
chortled to Reising. "Look, Leaky Peg! He is writing
mash-notes to Leaky Peg! This beats Lady Marie."

"I rather think it does," Hudson said, folding the
letters into his pocket. "Of course, Leaky Peg would most

emphatically deny anything of the sort, as would the others, if it were mentioned without Lady Marie's letters also being published. He has either written to them all, or to none. It's up to you."

"Then he's written to them all!" Alistair declared.

Reising frowned at him. "I'll be in touch," he said to Hudson.

"I'll be waiting at the Cat's Paw," Hudson replied.

"Fellows hasn't a chance after this!" Alistair crowed to his manager when Hudson had left them.

"Don't be a fool!" Reising told him. "Sir John won't let us publish now. What we must decide is whether to go ahead without his knowledge or tell him what Hudson has come up with. How badly do you want to get elected?"

"I don't want to do anything behind Sir John's back," Alistair said at once, shocked at such ungentlemanly conduct, for he was only a novice politician. "Certainly we must tell him exactly what Hudson means to do."

"I think we must. He has influence. He's too powerful a man to cross. We'll dump it in his lap and let him decide."

Sir John decided without much hesitation that the letters to his wife must be suppressed. He had not greatly favored the idea in the first place, but agreed to it as a last resort to keep patronage within the Tory ranks.

"You're out of pocket seven hundred and fifty pounds," Reising reminded him, hoping against hope to go ahead with the distribution of the letters that were stored in Sir John's own attic.

"It's only money. There will be other elections." He took the originals of his wife's letters along with the two boxes of pamphlets and consigned every last scrap of them to the flames. Then he sent a despondent Reising and

Alistair away to scour the town for a single low woman
with a letter from Fellows for sale. They wouldn't have
had time to get it published in volume in any case, but
they wanted to be doing something. They had no luck,
and when they had seen Hudson and gone their separate
ways to bed, they had tacitly conceded victory on the
morrow to Fellows.

At Ashley Hall, Lady Marie received the dressing-down
of her life for her loose conduct with every scarecrow and
mushroom for miles around. It was the only pleasure Sir
John had for his seven hundred and fifty pounds.

He had lost out on the bridge contract, but he sat for
an hour figuring out who would be giving the plum of
the improved road surfaces that would be done to ac-
commodate the new bridge. A Whig member did not mean
a Whig would have the final say so when it was the
Tories that were in power, and before retiring he wrote
a nice note to several influential gentlemen, inviting them
to spend a weekend at Ashley Hall. If all else failed and
Fellows actually got the reins in his own hands, well at
least he was fond of Lady Marie.

*14*

REISING and Alistair knew they had lost the election, but their smiling faces on the day before it took place gave no indication of it. They were in the village as usual, pumping hands, buying drinks and decrying the tolls on the bridge and carrying on very much as usual.

Putting a good face on their defeat, as Tony smilingly pointed out to his whipper-in.

The Whig candidate didn't slacken off his campaigning either, and had in fact a new chore to occupy him— flirting with everyone in the village who wore a skirt. Hudson was happy indeed that this business of romance had not arisen sooner; one day of it was more than enough. It was of course Fellow's believing that all the girls were jealous that led to this folly. Widows, wives, harlots and the visiting nuns from St. Mary's Priory— all were treated to his heavy-handed gallantry, till in desperation Hudson steered him to the tavern at the Cat's Paw. The way he was setting about it, he might yet manage to alienate every vote in the town.

Basingstoke and Allingham rode over in the afternoon, to remain at the abbey overnight and be on hand for the morrow's voting. Hudson swiftly consigned Basingstoke to the same intellectual level as Tony, and while those two longheaded gentlemen sat together over glasses of ale and complimented themselves on the clever way they had put one over on the Tories, Hudson and Allingham discussed their involvement in the bridge project and the scurrilous behavior of Sir John in planning to use his wife's letters.

The next morning bright and early, the four were up and dressed in their finest daytime regalia, the whipper-in and his candidate having their ensembles topped off by Saunders's hats, which near-totally ruined the effect. The three who had votes went immediately to the poll and cast them, while Hudson mentally assigned the votes of the others there to Whig or Tory, as he figured them likely to vote. Alistair and Reising were on hand as well, still putting a good face on their defeat.

The day was as good as a general holiday. Farmers, squires, gentlemen and a good many women swarmed in the main street of Crockett, making it a gay, carnival affair. Gingerbread stands and other stalls for the dispensing of refreshments were set up for, as on any holiday, the revelers wanted a constant supply of food and drink.

Martha Monteith normally would not allow her charges to be in the town on such a day of mischief-making as an election day was certain to be, but as the ladies had seen no more of the two gentlemen than a five-minute call just before dinner the preceding day, she relented and took them into Crockett herself to watch the goings-on.

She was so well pleased when Lord Allingham singled her out for special recognition, walking her to a bench protected from the chill winds by a canopy and procuring her a cup of coffee, that she quite lost track of her charges. Sara nipped immediately over to the Tory camp, but even this desertion was not noticed, and for a quarter of an hour Miss Monteith the younger assured Mr. Alistair that he was certain to win, for his pamphlet was so clever she couldn't understand a word of it and no one had been throwing potatoes at him for ages and ages. He confessed to her and no other soul in the village that his chances for victory were not great.

"You mean you won't have to go to London?" she asked joyfully, and was assured that this was the case. "Oh, I'm so glad," she breathed with an ecstatic sigh.

"Did you not want me to win?" Alistair asked, confused.

"More than anything in the world, but I'm very glad you won't have to leave Crockett."

He accepted these contradictory statements with a lover-to-be's broad understanding, and didn't even find them silly. Sara was so lovely and charming that he was not completely desolate to be staying at Crockett.

Miss Watters looked in vain for Mr. Hudson. He was nowhere to be seen. Fellows, his eyes alert for any lady he had not yet honored with a kind word, picked her out and strode up to her, smiling.

"I daresay you've come to congratulate me, Miss Watters."

"I hope I have occasion to congratulate you before many hours are out," she told him. "Where is Mr. Hudson today? I was sure he would be here today of all days."

"I've not seen hide nor hair of him. He says there are a good number of brown bags being passed around— Tory bags. He went into the back alley to see if he could find where Reising is hiding them. It ain't the bags he's worried about, of course, but what's in them."

"What *is* in them?" Lillian inquired with interest.

"Liquor."

Lillian looked in the direction of the closest alley.

"You won't see him there, Miss Watters. He's gone to represent me at Armstrong's funeral. One of us had to go. He'll be back before too long, for he told me to stay here in the village and not do anything foolish. It ain't over yet, though between you and me and the bedpost, Reising is wasting his blunt in giving away liquor, for half the fellows with brown bags have already voted. Pity old Armstrong went and cocked up his toes before he got around to vote. If I'd thought of it, I'd have had Isaac cast his vote, for he is the old man's heir and could have done it very likely, only I ain't at all sure he's on the list. They're very snifty about being on the list before they let you vote. However, I think they could have made an exception for my secretary. Isaac has the post, and his uncle is to help out on the farm, so he shan't be missed there. I gave him the post and didn't get a thing for it, not a single vote. Matt says it will pay off in the long run, and is writing up a dandy eulogy for Isaac to put into the local paper, telling everyone all about me. Well, he's not a well set-up chap, young Armstrong, and blind as a bat, but he'll do well enough for a pencil pusher. I'll have a deal of correspondence to be scribbled up and can't be wasting my precious time at that nonsense. I'll be at meetings and sittings of Parliament and all that."

"You will be missed in Crockett," Lillian said for the sake of civility.

"Aye, they'll have no one here to handle things for them. It's a pity, but I don't mean to be one of those fellows who never darken the door of the House now I am a Member of Parliament. I must be where things are going on, in the halls of power. I have to let them know how wide-awake we are here in Crockett, with the first suspension bridge in England—the Fellows Bridge—and if they think to go calling it the War Memorial Bridge or the Wellington Bridge or the Waterloo Bridge or anything of the sort, they're in for a stiff fight, I can tell you. Allingham is beginning to talk up changing the name. He was never too clever, to tell the truth. I never paid any heed to him. Basingstoke is awake on all suits, but Allingham is a bit soft in the head you know."

He then recalled that he had not complimented Miss Watters or made love to her, and he squared his shoulders to do his duty. "Well, you are looking pretty as a picture today, Miss Watters. Put them all to the blush with that old green hat. Looks very nice on you, 'pon my word."

"Thank you," she answered in a choked voice. "I am pleased you like my old green hat."

"It does well enough for an older woman like yourself. Miss Sara, of course, or one of the pretty young chicks wouldn't be caught in such a rig, but for an older woman it looks very well. A very nice hat indeed. Saunders couldn't do better."

At this point, Mr. Hudson, returned from the funeral, came up to Fellows and Lillian. "Are you making up to my girl, Tony?" he asked with a quizzing smile.

"Your girl? Matthew, you don't mean to say you and Miss Watters . . . Oh, you're bamming me! As if you'd look twice at . . . Heh heh, all a hum, I daresay. He is always joking, Miss Watters. A regular jokesmith, this chap."

"Mr. Fellows has just been admiring my old green quiz of a hat," Lillian said.

"Stealing a march on me! You want to watch this one; he's a very devil with the ladies. But you will please to leave the complimenting of Miss Watters to me, Tony."

"Very happy to, I'm sure," he answered ungallantly. "Well, so you're sparking Miss Sara's cousin, eh? Politics makes strange bedfellows."

"Pretty good ones, I think," Hudson answered, while Miss Watters's face turned noticeably red from holding in her mirth.

"As to that, the proof of the pudding is in the eating," Fellows said, with a critical look at Lillian.

"There is Miss Ratchett making eyes at you, Tony," Hudson said. "She'll be jealous if she sees you flirting with Miss Watters. The ladies, you know, are all consumed with jealousy. You'd better run along and tell her how pretty she looks in her red bonnet."

"Yes, by Jove, *there's* a girl knows how to dress," he said, and he dashed off to admire Miss Ratchett and be admired by her.

"I suppose he's stolen your heart away with his cunning praise," Hudson said.

"There ought to be a law against sending such a man as that to Parliament!" Lillian declared.

"Sharp as a tack."

"I don't know how you've stood it without murdering him during this entire month."

"Ah well, politics makes strange bedfellows," he said with a wicked gleam in his eyes. "He forgot to tell me that now I have made my bed, I must lie in it." He began looking around as though trying to find someone.

"Who is it you are looking for?" she asked him.

"I'm not looking for anyone. I've found you. I was just wondering if there was somewhere we could go."

Lillian was quite overcome, not only at the words—for it was clearly not just a bench or a tent for a cup of coffee he had in mind—but at the warm tone in which they were spoken and the glowing eyes of the speaker. Although they looked around quite thoroughly, there was no convenient place for them to go to be alone, which she felt sure was what he had in mind. The town was a perfect wall of people, noise and confusion.

"Looks like we'll have to wait," he said, frowning in frustration. "I think you know, in any case, what I want to say to you."

Lillian was in much of a mind to hear it, and thought the noise provided enough privacy even for a proposal of marriage. "No. What *did* you want to say?"

"It was more something I wanted to do, actually," he replied, focusing his eyes on her lips for a noticeable minute. She almost thought he was going to do it, right in the middle of the crowded town. But he looked up and smiled instead, then looked around again. "The party's beginning to get rough."

"It is all those brown bags Reising is dispensing in the back alleys."

"The ones Hudson is dispensing are probably even more to blame. I didn't cut mine with water, as I think Reising did. I had a swig from one of his and I'm pretty sure he had diluted it."

"The cheapskate!"

"Keeping all the good stuff for himself. What can you expect of a Tory? Well, from whatever source, the liquor has been flowing pretty freely, and it's time Miss Monteith—notice I am not presuming to call her Aunt Martha yet—takes you two buds home. By this evening it will be bedlam. I hope you don't mean to return then."

"Not when we are being hinted away so very broadly. I suppose you will be here?"

"I must keep a sharp eye on the counting. Reising is up to every dirty trick in the book."

"I have a feeling poor Mr. Reising has been sadly traduced throughout this whole affair."

"He's not a bad sort, but I mean to keep on my guard till after the counting. I'll be here till all hours. I won't see you till tomorrow. I seem to be always saying that, don't I? You'll think me a poor wooer, never spending an evening with you, but if wishes were horses, as our friend says, your saloon would be a veritable stable. I suppose Aunt Martha might not like that."

"I daresay *Miss Monteith* might take exception to it."

"I don't think Sara would mind," he answered, unrepentant.

"How soon will Mr. Fellows go to London, if he wins?" Lillian inquired, acknowledging herself bested in the matter of names.

"In a day or two. I thought I'd get stuck to take him all the way—I daren't let him go alone. God knows what hobble he'd fall into along the way—but Henderson, one of our M.P.'s, is to meet us at Devizes, just east of Bath, and take him off my hands. I'll pass the bullwhip over to him, along with dire warnings regarding the degree of watching he requires. With his new romantic role to live up to, he'd go trailing into Whitehall with a lightskirt on either wing. I shouldn't be gone longer than two days."

"Two days," she repeated. It seemed an eternity, and she sincerely hoped he would find a moment's privacy to put the question to her before he left.

Taking her arm, he walked her toward Martha, and Allingham too pointed out the number of men already weaving and becoming unruly. Martha took the hint, and shepherded her two charges to the carriage, under the aegis of Lord Allingham and Cecilford's heir. The only thing lacking was Mr. Fellows for Sara, but she was beginning to give up on him; he had been ogling Miss Ratchett so obviously the last few days that Sara's real beau was beginning to be acknowledged, and forgiven for being a Tory.

Affairs in the village took a rapid turn for the wilder not long after the ladies left, but despite that, the counting of the votes was a sober, serious affair, and no considerable quantity of drink was allowed to those involved. Hudson drank three cups of coffee, but nothing stronger till the votes were counted, and Fellows assured of a victory too wide to be subject to recounting, after which he added yet another crime to his career, and became quite pleasantly foxed, but not so foxed that he failed to get Fellows booked into a room at the Cat's Paw first. It was too late, and they were all too tired to go to the abbey. There was some little difficulty keeping a certain lady of the night out of Tony's room, for he seemed as eager for her company as was she for his. Hudson slipped her a folded bill and a wink, mentioning a room number at random. When she found it to be occupied by the only respectable couple honouring the inn with their presence that evening, she was not too sorry to have got her pay without performing her duties. They lost Basingstoke along the way to the muslin company, but the Honorable Member was saved from disgrace, and castigated his rescuers as cupboard Tories for their trouble, saving all the goodies for themselves.

Early in the morning, after Allingham, Basingstoke, Fellows and Alistair were all abed, the whippers-in met in Hudson's room to share a bottle of undiluted brandy. Their duties done to the best of their respective abilities, they got their heads together for a very pleasant rehashing of the campaign.

"They stuck us with a pair of rare boys this time, old friend," Reising said. "Here's to 'em." They lifted their glasses and drank.

"Mine was a fool, you know," Reising confessed.

"Mine made him appear a wizard," Hudson replied, glad to be able to say it aloud at last.

"Aye, there was little enough to choose between them. Yours was an old fool and mine a young one. He's done nothing but moon about since the pretty young lady took a shine to him. Did you put her up to it then?"

"No. I'd have preferred she wait till the election was over."

"I didn't know whether to encourage him in it or hold him back, not knowing what you were up to. I doubted she could really be as dumb as she seemed and feared you had some card up your sleeve. And then once Telford came I lost my boy entirely. He jawed my ear off with talk of cantilevers and suspension cables and clearances till I began to think he was running for county engineer instead of M.P."

"I still think you had the best of it. Mine doesn't know yet whether he's a Whig or a Tory."

"Whatever he is, he's rich at least. Alistair ain't, and we had to depend on old Sinclair."

"Mine ain't much poorer than when he started. I've seen rocks bleed freer."

They congratulated and consoled each other and ran down their candidates for an hour, parting the best of friends.

"Will I be seeing you in Burridge in two months' time for the next by-election?" Reising asked. "Our member there is on the point of sticking his fork in the wall. We figure two months till the election."

"As it's another Tory stronghold, you'll be seeing me there," Hudson replied.

"It's au revoir then," Reising said, and walked from the room with a fairly steady step.

*15*

A public meeting was to take place the next day on the village green, where a dais had been erected. The candidates were to meet and publicly shake hands and declare each other fine fellows. The star of the show was Anthony Fellows Esq., M.P. for Crockett. Hudson had written him a modest victory speech and practiced him up on it before herding him to the green. For this occasion he was allowed to exchange his politicking hat for his own, more becoming, Baxter. The occasion was dignified by formal clothing for those to sit on the dais. Everyone—including the ladies from New Moon—was present at the meeting.

It was remarkable to see foolish Tony Fellows looking so dignified and intelligent. A well-cut black suit did wonders for him. He spoke the words of his mentor without a hitch or a flaw, thanked everyone for every imaginable thing, and even thanked those who had voted against him for adhering to their principles. It had taken quite a few rehearsals to prevent his describing those principles as repressive and reactionary, but at last Hudson had succeeded. Mr. Alistair too made a speech, almost as fine as Tony's but of less interest to everyone except Sara as he was in no position to do anyone any favors. It was the general opinion that they need not be ashamed to send Mr. Fellows to London to represent them. A very fine, sensible man he had always been, they all agreed, as they didn't really know him well at all. Miss Ratchett measured him through narrowed eyes and decided he would have to do. His abbey lent him a certain *éclat* in the town, and in the city an Honorable Member must surely move in the first circles. In any case, she could not be choosy. There were few gentlemen in Crockett, and Papa refused to take her to London to choose from a wider field.

Mr. Hudson stayed very much in the background, very dignified himself with his black coat and black hair, ennobled at the temples with the wings of gray. Lillian always felt she was looking at a judge when she regarded him, and smiled to herself to think of that noble-looking gentleman pulling the barn door off its hinges, scrambling around to bribe Leaky Peg, and bringing in his flash culls to perform any deeds beyond his own considerable powers of criminality.

There was first a spate of merrymaking on the green, with free food and beverages—the last of the bribes served to everyone—while the band played away in the background. After this general celebration, certain chosen persons were invited to the abbey for a more refined party. Mr. Fellows was vehemently against feeding Tories in his own home, but gentle insistence from all his mentors eventually succeeded in his allowing at least Mr. Alistair and Reising to come. Without Fellows's knowledge, an invitation was also extended to Sir John and Lady Marie by Allingham, who counted on Sir John's sense of propriety to stay away, as indeed he did.

Miss Ratchett succeeded pretty well in monopolizing Mr. Fellows's attention, for no one else really wanted it. Sara followed Alistair around like a puppy, and Miss Watters was lucky to get a look at Mr. Hudson; he was so busy attending to all the up-coming business for the riding that Mr. Fellows should have been seeing to. He hardly looked at Lillian, and she began to wonder if she had imagined all those intimate glances he had been casting her way, and all the suggestive remarks he had made. She knew he was leaving the next day, yet despite that he disappeared into a study with Allingham several hours. When he came out, he was pulled right into the middle of a group petitioning for federal moneys to set up a hospital.

It was nearly time for them to leave before she had a

minute with him, and Fellows chose that very moment to accost his whipper-in and thank him for lending a hand with the campaign.

"You did a dashed good job, Matt, and I won't hesitate to acknowledge to anyone who asks me that without your help I wouldn't have had such a whopping majority." He had squeeked in with a whopping majority of fifty votes, but in a small riding fifty votes was not subject to recount, and so it was a nominal whopping victory. "I won't insult my constituents to suggest they wouldn't have had the sense to elect a Whig, for they would and we all know it, but the fact of the matter is I give you credit for the size of my majority. You are a dashed knowing one; Basingstoke I think will agree with me on that, and if you ever come a cropper, I'll find a spot for you on my staff. I have young Armstrong, an orphan you know and not fit for real work, to rattle off my letters for me, but there's always a place for good men like yourself in the party. I wouldn't hesitate to recommend you to anyone to give him a hand with his campaign."

"Thank you, Tony. I appreciate the recommendation."

"No more than the simple truth. I hope I ain't too proud to allow you was a little help to me. In fact, I'll drop a word in Brougham's ear when I get to London, and have him look out for a soft spot for you in the City. At your age you must be fagged to death being an errand boy for us members."

"I do begin to find it wearing," Hudson admitted, and was assured again that Fellows would put in a word for him in the right quarters.

Lillian had some hopes Mr. Hudson would find time to look for a quiet spot before she left—and in an abbey with fifty rooms it seemed possible he might succeed. But when it was time for her to go, all she could do was congratulate him on the miracle he had performed.

"Getting him elected, you mean?"

"No, not wringing his neck for giving you so little credit."

Although he shook her hand with a hard squeeze and said he'd see her tomorrow, her hopes plunged. She had to make do with reading into that single grip of the hand all the tender words she had been anticipating. Never was a handshake considered in such minute detail, and seldom must one have given so little pleasure.

She didn't get much more of his company when he and Tony stopped at New Moon the next morning on their way to Devizes. The full quorum of ladies was present—Aunt Martha, Lady Monteith, Sara and Lillian. One day's congratulations to the incumbent was not enough; he had to be congratulated again and again by them all. He never tired of hearing himself mentioned as the Honorable Member, and to his elation the ladies repeated it to his heart's content. Nor did he take it as an offense when Sara, in an excess of reverence, called him Sir Anthony. A milord or a your grace would also have gone down very well, but he could wait till he was knighted for those promotions.

Much as he enjoyed strutting before the ladies, he could hardly wait to get to London, where he fancied the House must be on tiptoe to meet him, and e'er long he was urging Hudson out the door, calling him "my good man," and not Matt, now that he was raised to his new office. Matthew expected to be reduced to "Hudson" by the time he got rid of him at Devizes.

"We must be off," Fellows said at last. "I have a dozen matters to bring to Brougham's attention. Can't waste a minute. Waste not, want not, you know."

Hudson looked at Lillian and smiled. "I'll be returning soon," he said, her only hint that there was unfinished business between them.

"Soon? No such thing," Fellows objected. "Can't be poking back here every two days. The House is in session."

"*I* will be returning," Hudson said.

"What the deuce for? I'll get you a spot, my good man. I told you I'd speak to Brougham."

"I really don't think that will be necessary, Tony, but in any case I'm not going all the way to London just now."

"Oh—I see how it is," Fellows declared in loud, significant tones. "*Amor omnia vincit,* eh?"

"Just so," Hudson agreed quietly.

"Which reminds me, old chap, we must nip in and say au revoir to the Ratchetts."

"Yes, you will want to take your leave of Miss Ratchett," Hudson said, risking a glance at Miss Watters.

"Ha ha, I've done you out on her, true enough. But I daresay it is my being an M.P. that gives me the preference, for it was pretty warm with you two for a while there."

"Perhaps I ought to have a few words with *Mr.* Ratchett," Hudson said, and got the M.P. out the door before Lillian quite threw a fit.

"Well, they're gone," Martha said, and everyone looked to her for elaboration, for she was not one to waste words on the obvious.

"I'm certainly glad it isn't Mr. Alistair who must go to London," Sara said with a shiver at the close escape.

"The two of them got away without a single offer. I hope you can manage to bring Mr. Alistair up to scratch, Sara, for you've lost Mr. Fellows," Martha continued. "That Miss Ratchett will not be so backward when they call on her. And you, Lillian, must get back home and attach Mr. Thorstein. Mr. Hudson won't be back."

"He said he would come back!"

"They always *say* they will come back to effect a graceful exit. He won't be back."

"Why should he say so if he doesn't mean it?" Melanie inquired.

"Because he didn't want to make Lillian look a fool and himself a jilt, which is what he is. He'll drop a note claiming business that has delayed him—the necessity for going on all the way to London or some such thing. Then it will be a postscript on one of Fellows's letters describing more delays, and that'll be the end of it. Next thing we'll hear of that one will be of his engagement to some fine lady. He would have made a fine *partie,* Cecilford's heir, but there is some little quirk in him I cannot quite trust. A man who will countenance bribery and trickery as he did is not to be depended on. It is the way of men's world. Now don't mope, Lillian. He's had a dozen chances to offer for you if it was his intention. Haven't you driven with him twice and been at balls and parties and meetings a dozen times? No, he was amusing himself, and I believe he has left Miss Ratchett with her heart on her sleeve as well, but she will settle for Mr. Fellows, and he is plenty good enough for her too. Too good. We shan't let you be made a laughingstock by him. Back to Yorkshire, and you'll be engaged to Mr. Thorstein before we read of Mr. Hudson's marriage."

Martha spoke thus to prepare Lillian for the worst, but actually she had no notion of leaving before the day which should see Mr. Hudson return—with a few days' grace thrown in on account of his being Cecilford's heir. If he came back, so much the better; if he didn't, she had prepared the girl for it. What more could she do? She was hoping as hard as Lillian herself that he would come, and decided to count on it sufficiently to allow her to begin considering alternative brides for Mr. Thorstein. There was Cousin Philmont's middle daughter, elbowing her way past twenty and no one in sight . . . she would be a congenial replacement for Lillian. Still, just enough uncertainty clung about Hudson that she didn't write to Mrs. Philmont yet.

The next two days passed quickly for three of the four ladies at New Moon. Mr. Alistair came and had private words with Lady Monteith. As well ask a cat or a dog as Lady Monteith what he had said, but when she muttered something about a house his father was giving him, and two thousand pounds a year—or maybe it was two thousand acres—Martha assumed he had asked permission to pay his addresses to Sara, and gave her own permission as soon as he returned.

The family was later informed in no uncertain terms by her that it was a very fine estate (with two thousand acres, not pounds), and the income was twenty-five hundred a year. The marriage would be before Christmas, and Martha wouldn't be able to come all the way from Yorkshire for it, so she would take Sara shopping and buy her trousseau for a wedding gift before she left. No furs or feathers, mind, but a half-dozen good, dark, sober matron's gowns for the youthful bride. She thought privately that it was a pity she couldn't be in touch with Mr. Thorstein for the acquisition of the woolens.

Sara's little mouth turned down, but Lillian whispered to her that Aunt Martha wasn't such a dragon as she let on, and she could have any color gowns she wanted.

"It's feathers I wanted," she said, a tear trembling in her lucid blue eye.

"Buy them yourself, goose! They only cost a shilling."

This ingenious idea brought back her smiles. "You're so clever," she said admiringly. "I hope Mr. Hudson comes back and marries you."

"So do I," Lillian replied, and was surprised at herself for admitting it to a single soul.

"He's clever too. My, what a hard time you will have understanding each other."

Two days had never seemed so long to Mr. Hudson. Tony Fellows had been hard enough to endure, but a condescending elected Member of Parliament was utterly insupportable. Hudson finally gave him a couple of sharp dressing-downs, after which Fellows addressed him again as Matt. At Devizes, Hudson unloaded the member on to Mr. Henderson with a vast sigh of relief.

"The election was an upset," Henderson said. "Very good for party morale. It must have been an interesting campaign."

"A regular one," Hudson answered indifferently.

"How about our new member?" Fellows had gone to the desk at the inn to make himself known in all his glory, and thus the other gentlemen were free to discuss him.

"He'll look well enough on the back bench, as long as we keep his mouth closed."

"A dud, is he? Why did they run him? Is he rich?"

"Fairly, but I had to wrestle him to the ground and squeeze every pound out of him. He has an heiress in his eye, however, whose Papa is much more generous. Name of Ratchett. They'll come down heavy if it is a match."

"I'll prod him along then."

"I'd appreciate it if Brougham would see him for a few minutes. He has the idea they're to be bosom beaux, and it would be nice if he at least got to shake hands with the boss."

"I'll see to it. We'll get notices in the *Gazette* and the *Observer*. Something about some new kind of a bridge, isn't there?"

"Yes, mention that. I've already sent in one piece, but the more coverage we can get out of it the better."

"No excitement at all in the campaign?"

"Not much, but there was an interesting sidelight."

"What's that?"

"I've found myself a wife."

"Have you, by God! I hope she'll make us a good Whig hostess?"

"She could if she would, but I'm not sure she will."

"Much chance she'll have not to!" Henderson laughed.

"I'll take care to keep you away from her. A fine idea she'll have of me if she hears you talk like that."

"Somebody should warn her," Henderson roasted him, and asked him a few pertinent questions regarding the lady's background. He was a little surprised to hear that

Hudson hadn't looked higher for a wife than an unknown Miss Watters from Yorkshire, but was naturally too polite to say so and assumed the lady must have some exceptional degree of beauty to have snared the elusive Hudson.

*16*

❧❧❧❧❧❧❧❧❧❧❧❧❧❧❧❧❧❧❧❧❧❧❧❧❧❧❧❧❧❧

ALISTAIR rapidly became a fixture at New Moon. With all the spare time fallen on his hands since the campaign was over, he didn't know what to do with himself, and as his reception there was as royal as three delighted ladies could make it, he stayed from morning till dark, with occasional excursions to the Fellows Bridge. Sara was coming to learn that it was a pretty good sort of bridge after all. William had told her all about it, and drawn her a picture that rested in her treasure box with her pamphlet from the campaign as testimonials to William's worth.

He was there when Mr. Hudson returned, on the very day promised, and that little quirk Martha could not quite like dropped away from him like magic. It was not only Lillian's heart that leapt when he walked into the room, for Martha had also been on tenterhooks wondering if he would come.

Almost before anyone had asked him about the trip and how Tony was liking being an M.P., Sara gave him her news. "We are getting married too, me and William, Mr. Hudson. He asked me right after you left."

"Congratulations! I'm very happy to hear it. It doesn't come as a complete surprise to me," Hudson said, then added, "Did you say you are getting married *too*? Is someone else getting married?"

There was an awkward pause. Both Martha and Lillian feared—were virtually certain in fact—that she referred to her cousin and Cecilford's heir, with never an offer from him! Sara blinked her big blue eyes. "Aren't you— that is—" She stopped dead for time. "William and I are to be married before Christmas. I'm getting six new gowns from Aunt Martha," she finally got out, and the bad moment was over.

Martha promptly chided her for being a peagoose, and her mama said boldly that indeed she was not. She had got quite short with Martha now that she had Sara's groom to defend her.

Still there lingered an uneasiness, a feeling that Hudson was there to claim a bride, and that Sara might any moment break out with more embarrassing statements. All the ladies except Lillian kept looking at Hudson expectantly, as though waiting for him to go down on bended knee and say his piece, or at least pull a diamond out of his pocket. Lillian felt all the lively discomfort of being unasked, made tolerable only by the sure feeling that she would be asked as soon as that private spot could be reached.

But how could it be done? It was nearly five o'clock when Hudson arrived, an inconvenient hour. He could not ask her out for a drive, for besides the time there was a howling wind blowing and considerable rain falling. To arise and suddenly ask to see her alone seemed a gauche thing, so the group chatted on, while Melanie began to get fidgety and wonder if she should invite Mr. Hudson to stay to dinner. Odd Martha had not attended to it. She rather disliked to usurp her place.

Martha's mind was tending in a different direction from dinner. Hudson was not to be allowed to get away again without coming up to scratch, and she felt that all that was lacking was the opportunity.

"Well, Lillian," she said, taking the bit in her teeth, "why don't you and Mr. Hudson go out for a little drive? You have time before dinner. I hope you will stay to dinner, Mr. Hudson?"

"It's five to five!" Lady Monteith proclaimed in dismay. Did this mean dinner would be put off? She was starved.

"It's pouring rain!" Sara put in in her usual helpful fashion.

"Mr. Hudson has just got here from driving all day," Mr. Alistair contributed.

"Nonsense, it's just a shower," Martha said. "Lillian doesn't mind a little rain. It's a fine day."

This had a Fellowish sound to it, and the frustrated lovers exchanged a secret smile. Sara caught them out in it and clapped her hands in glee. "I see what it is!" she fairly shouted. "Yes, indeed—Lillian *loves* the rain and wet!"

Before she could say more, Hudson cut in. "Let's go, shall we, Miss Watters?"

"What about dinner?" Melanie demanded petulantly.

Martha still had enough authority to silence her with a glance. Lillian went for her pelisse, Hudson to order his carriage, and Martha ran for an umbrella, for going out in the rain was really a thing she disliked very much, for herself or her nieces.

Once they were safely out of the house, Hudson said, "Now where do we go? It seems there is no such a thing as a private place for us in the whole town."

"The grave's a fine and private place," Lillian suggested, laughing in relief at getting away.

"But none, I think, do there embrace," he added. "That wouldn't do for us, my coy mistress. You see what evil design I have in mind. We'll have to make do with the carriage. Or would you prefer to walk, as you like the rain so much?"

With the wind lashing at her coat and the rain streaking her face, she took this for a joke, and they entered the carriage.

"What a hard girl you are to see alone for a minute," he said, and even as he spoke their privacy was invaded. A dark form huddled into a coat was coming up the drive, his head bent into the wind. "That's Armstrong, isn't it?" Hudson asked.

It was indeed Armstrong, wending his way home from

the newspaper office and seeking shelter from the storm till the rain should let up.

"You'll catch your death of cold, Mr. Armstrong," Lillian said. "Mr. Hudson, could we not bring him home?"

Hudson frowned at her heavily, but Isaac answered for him. "No, it is too far out of your way. I only meant to stop for shelter till 5:30, when Mr. Hicks will be going my way; he always takes me up. I meant to be back at the roadside in time to meet him."

"Do you mean to say you *walk* to work in the village?" Hudson asked.

"The horse is needed on the farm," Isaac explained, looking guilty about the whole thing.

"Fellows has his stable full of nags. Take one; he won't be here to need them."

"I couldn't take his horse without asking him."

"He asked me to tell you that he wouldn't want his secretary going about on foot," Hudson lied. This was the way Fellows would be talked into agreeing with it. It would detract from his own consequence to have a secretary too poor to ride.

Isaac had got into the carriage, and it was decided he would be driven to the village to meet Mr. Hicks there. Never one to waste a minute, Hudson used the time to give him all the instructions Fellows had failed to give him regarding his duties, urging him to be in touch with Allingham if any crisis arose and not to go to Basingstoke.

"I'm very glad you told me, sir, for to tell the truth, Mr. Fellows didn't make my duties very clear."

"He was pretty busy," Hudson said dryly.

Before long Armstrong was being let off at the stable-yard to join Mr. Hicks. Hudson turned to Lillian with an intent light in his eyes, and about his lips a quiet smile of anticipation about to be fulfilled.

"Now, Miss Watters, did you miss me at all?"

"Yes, it seemed very quiet with you and Mr. Fellows gone and the election all over."

"How much did you miss me?" he asked, ignoring everything but her affirmative.

"Quite a lot," she answered.

"Oh you wretched, rockhearted woman! Is that all? I have missed you forty-eight hours a day. More—two hundred and forty. Every hour seemed like ten away from you. I have been gone three weeks." His arms went out in an instinctive gesture to seize her, but a curious pair of eyes peering in at the window reminded him that this was no very private place, and he laughed forlornly. He moved from his side of the carriage to join her, taking both her hands in a firm grip. "It seems hard to me that after waiting a month and three weeks I still have to go on waiting."

"You are exaggerating greatly, Mr. Hudson."

"You may, and I hope will, stop calling me Mr. Hudson as though we were mere acquaintances. My name is Matthew, and I am averse to neither Matt nor even some more intimate term of endearment, as there is just a touch of the foot-scraper in that particular nickname that rather irks me. And I am not exaggerating in the least, but understating the case."

"You didn't care for me when first you came here, so don't let on you did. You sat with Sara all the first evening, and many subsequent evenings as well."

"For a half-hour the first evening I thought her prettier, till she began regaling me with tales of Peter

Pepper and his pampered pups, or some such thing. As soon as she said you had such books too, all about laughing ladies, I knew I must get on terms with you. There could not be two such charming fools as Sara in one place, and I suspected at once you were a hussy, to be teasing the poor ninny so."

"You have a shocking memory! It was not pampered pups but pink-plumed parakeets. And I *have* such a book too! All about the campaign, about the Whig whip who whisks into . . ." She stopped, having run out of words.

"Pucker your gorgeous lips once more and you'll get yourself kissed, my girl," he warned.

"It was not nice of you to tease me and pretend you thought me prettier after taking her to dinner at our harvest ball."

"To stop her trailing after Alistair. How many explanations must I make about that night? Well, she has a lovely facade, like a big full moon shining in a spring sky, promising romance but not delivering. To me, in any case. I find her cold, and you know my penchant for sunshine. Unlike yourself, who dote on wind and rain!" he added with a satirical glint in his eye.

"I do like rain," she responded.

"Good—we'll pray for a nice wet day in two weeks' time and get buckled, shall we?"

She listened starry-eyed, too happy to speak, and he went on. "You've seen me at my very worst, Lil, conniving and scheming and all the rest of it. That is only a small part of my life and will be no part of yours if you truly dislike it."

"I don't think I'd see much of my husband in that case," she ventured.

"Only ten or twelve hours a day."

"After you've got at that with your crooked arithmetic it would be one hour a day."

He smiled and glanced briefly out the carriage window, where Mr. Saunders was strolling by, peering into the carriage with the avid curiosity of the townsman who considers his neighbors' doings very much his own affair. "I have wanted to kiss you for ages," he said, "and nearly did, too, more than once. First when you accused me of dangling after Miss Ratchett at your aunt's tea party, and the night of the ball when you accused me—so unjustly!—of importing the dashers. The day of the election in the village you were within an ace of being thoroughly kissed in front of the whole of Crockett. Strange, it is usually your worst behavior that puts these ideas into my head."

"I have long suspected you to harbor an admiration for misconduct of any kind."

"We don't need the Honorable Member to remind us that birds of a feather flock together, do we? We don't need anyone but each other," he declared, and without further words he pulled her into his arms, to kiss her soundly before ever they were out of the town and to go on kissing her for half a mile down the road, while the storm howled outside, unheard by the acknowledged lover of tempests. He stopped for only a short interval to remove her bonnet and kiss her ears; then he looked up to wave at Mr. Bilkes as he passed them on his mount.

"I've just laid waste your reputation," he said, and seized her again to resume his evil activities, as she did not seem as disturbed by them as she ought to be.

"What fools we are!" Lillian said suddenly.

He looked a question at her. "We don't have to go

on living here, and in any case I hope I have made plain I mean to do the right thing by you."

"I'm not talking about that. I have just thought what we should have done about Fellows's letters to Lady Marie. We should have spoken to Basingstoke. I bet you *he* had answers from her we could have used. If she wrote to Fellows, she surely must have written to him. And as he still cared for her, he would have kept her letters too. You could have had your flash culls steal them. Matt, I'm ashamed of you! How came you not to think of such a thing?"

"Matt isn't really my favorite name."

"What has that got to do with anything?"

"You should ask me what I would like you to call me."

"But this other thing just popped into my head."

"Let it pop out again, wretch!" he commanded. "And never mind reading me any more lectures about my behavior, when you are a step ahead of me at every turn. Basingstoke didn't keep her letters. It occurred to me also, but too late."

"And another thing—the one you really ought to have run in this election is Mr. Ratchett."

"I know. I have regretted it since the moment I met him, but it was too late then too."

"He is a little bored, I think, since retiring, and besides having such a lot of money to throw around, he has his daughter."

"At least *I* didn't mention her!"

"She would like nothing better than to be a hostess, though she is excessively vulgar and would require a good deal of polishing-up."

"If she succeeds in nabbing Fellows, you can take her in hand."

"I will, to prevent you from doing it. Matthew, I was just thinking . . . at the next general election, do you think you could go to Yorkshire?"

"I don't have to ask why, do I?"

"I bet you could get our Whig candidate in. And really, you know, it is dreadful the way the textile workers are treated. The Tory candidate sent out scurrilous literature pretending his opponent was an atheist, and I think if you had been there to beat him up . . ."

"He should have been threatened with a libel suit."

"Well, you see, that was never mentioned at all! If *you* had been there . . ."

"Shut up, Lil," he said firmly. "I am glad you mean to help me, but I like to run my own show. There will be only one pair of trousers worn in our house."

"You will look very strange in skirts, Matt," she told him without a second's hesitation.

"Lil!" he said dangerously, but his laughing black eyes told her she need not fear his menacing tone.

"Don't think I am fooled into thinking you would disapprove of my wearing trousers. You have been offering me a pair since we first met practically."

"Oh no—if you are to be my accomplice in felony you must keep up an appearance of respectability. You mentioned it yourself—I thought it particularly astute of you. You stick to your petticoats and I'll continue to douse my hair with whitewash. I expect it is coming out with all this rain."

"Matthew!" She stared at his hair in fascination, and to be sure, the wings were less gray than formerly. "Oh, you *sneak!*" she gasped, then burst into a fit of giggles.

"You didn't tumble to it? I thought I saw you

looking at my hair rather closely, but perhaps you were just admiring it?"

"I shouldn't be surprised at anything you do, but I must confess this takes the cake. You letting on to be an old man!"

"The pretense is over. I am but a young man, and an impatient young man at that. Come here and kiss me, you hussy. That's an order."

They were so close a piece of thin paper couldn't have been wedged between them, so she had only to comply with the latter of his demands, and even that token of obedience was not necessary as the impatient young man resumed kissing her instead.